Danny Blackgoat: Rugged Road to Freedom

Tim Tingle

7th Generation
Summertown, Tennessee

7th Generation, an imprint of
Book Publishing Company
PO Box 99, Summertown, TN 38483
888-260-8458
bookpubco.com
nativevoicesbooks.com

ISBN: 978-1-939053-05-3

19 18 17 16 15 14   1 2 3 4 5 6 7 8 9

Printed in the United States

Library of Congress Cataloging-in-Publication Data
Tingle, Tim.
  Danny Blackgoat : rugged road to freedom / Tim Tingle.
     pages cm. -- (Danny Blackgoat ; 2)
  Summary: Having escaped from Fort Davis, Texas, seventeen-year-old Danny
Blackgoat, a Navajo, must still face many obstacles in order to rescue his family
from Fort Sumner, New Mexico, and find freedom after the Long Walk of 1864.
  ISBN 978-1-939053-05-3 (pbk.) -- ISBN 978-1-939053-91-6 (e-book)
  1. Slave trade--West (U.S.)--Fiction. [1. Conduct of life--Fiction. 2. Navajo
Indians--Fiction. 3. Indians of North America--Texas--Fiction. 4. Adventure and
adventurers--Fiction. 5. Texas--History--19th century--Fiction. 6. New Mexico--
History--19th century--Fiction.] I. Title.
  PZ7.T489Dar 2014
  [Fic]--dc23
                                    2013042439

Book Publishing Company is a
member of Green Press Initiative.
We chose to print this title on paper
with 100% postconsumer recycled
content, processed without chlorine,
which saved the following natural
resources:
• 26 trees
• 824 pounds of solid waste
• 12,318 gallons of water
• 2,271 pounds of greenhouse gases
• 12 million BTU of energy

For more information on
Green Press Initiative, visit
www.greenpressinitiative.org.
Environmental impact estimates
were made using the Environmental
Defense Fund Paper Calculator.
For more information visit
www.papercalculator.org.

Contents

Dedication

To Lonnie and Martha Boggs, whose fine photography inspired the cover art for *Danny Blackgoat, Navajo Prisoner*.

Danny Blackgoat's story began in *Danny Blackgoat, Navajo Prisoner* and continues in *Danny Blackgoat: Rugged Road to Freedom*. Watch for the conclusion of Danny's adventures, coming soon!

Chapter 1
Surprise at the Water Hole

Winter, 1864

Fort Davis, Texas, a Civil War prison camp for captured rebel soldiers. With the help of Jim Davis, a fellow prisoner, Danny Blackgoat has escaped. Seventeen years old and Navajo, Danny is hoping to rejoin his family, who endured the Long Walk and are now struggling to survive at Fort Sumner, New Mexico.

"Everybody up!" shouted a guard. Sunrise at Fort Davis was still an hour away. The prisoners rolled and grumbled. Some rolled out of bed. Most rolled over and covered their heads with their pillows.

"Get up now!" the guard shouted. Two guards walked from bed to bed in the barracks. They prodded the prisoners with their rifle butts. When a guard came to Danny Blackgoat's bed, he paused. Danny was a young Navajo boy, the only Indian prisoner at the fort. He always slept under the covers, curled up like a snake.

"Well," he said, "looks like our troublemaker thinks he can sleep all day long."

He nudged the boy in the ribs. Danny didn't move. The guard flung back the covers. The bed was empty, except for a blanket rolled up to look like a body.

"Hey!" he shouted. "The Indian boy's gone!"

The other prisoners scrambled out of bed and surrounded Danny's cot.

"I knew you guards couldn't keep him here," said an older prisoner.

"He's smarter than all of you put together," said another.

The prisoners started talking to themselves, softly at first, and then they talked loud enough for every guard to hear. Some even yelled at the guards.

"Yeah, I hope he's never caught!" shouted a prisoner.

Soon all of the prisoners were cheering Danny Blackgoat.

"You thought he was a dumb Indian," said a young prisoner from Tennessee, "and he outsmarted you!"

The guards backed away. Four soldiers entered the barracks, led by an officer. They aimed their shotguns at the prisoners.

"Back to your beds," the officer shouted. "Sit down and keep your hands where we can see them. A prisoner has escaped. If you say another word or move suddenly, we will shoot you!"

By sunrise, Danny Blackgoat was already ten miles from Fort Davis, riding Fire Eye, his new horse. As the sun topped the mountains to the east, Danny came to a halt. He led Fire Eye away from the road and into a grove of scrubby trees.

"Take it easy, boy," he said in his Navajo language. A cloud rose from his mouth as he spoke. The air was freezing cold.

Fire Eye stomped the ground and shook his head. He was breathing hard. "We need to find some water," Danny said. He lifted himself high in the saddle and looked up and down the road. "Nobody's following us. We're safe for now," he whispered.

He would not be safe for long.

"Let's go, boy!" he said, patting Fire Eye on the neck. He urged his horse up the slope of a hill. From the top, Danny spotted a ranch less than a mile away. Surrounding the ranch, cattle grazed on the open plains.

Where there are cattle, Danny thought, *there must be water.*

He kept a sharp eye on the ranch house, looking for any sign of people. Seeing no one, he turned his gaze to the cattle. They gathered at the base of a hill, in a clump of dry mesquite trees.

That must be where the water is. Danny eased Fire Eye down the hill, staying as far away from the ranch house as possible. As he neared the cattle, he saw a bright puddle of water, bubbling from the rocks at the base of the hill.

"Ready to drink, Fire Eye? I'm thirsty, too," he said. The trees blocked the view from the ranch house, so Danny felt safe. He stepped from the saddle and took Fire Eye by the reins. "Easy, boy," he said. "These are only cattle. They won't hurt us."

Fire Eye saw the water and stomped the ground.

"I guess that means you like what you see," Danny said. "Here, let's get a drink." He cupped his hands and knelt by the spring. Fire Eye began to drink.

"Hey!"

Danny leaped to his feet. The shout came from the trees. He saw no one.

POW! A shotgun blasted a rock two feet from where Danny stood.

"What are you doing here?" the voice called out. A young boy, close to Danny's age, stepped from the shadows.

"We kill Indians when we see 'em," said the boy.

Danny backed away, holding his hands high.

"I don't want to hurt anybody," he said.

The boy crouched down and fumbled with his shotgun. "Don't move," he said.

He is reloading his shotgun, thought Danny. *He's going to shoot me.*

Danny jumped over the spring and ran to the crouching boy. He knocked the shotgun from his hands and shoved him hard. The boy landed on his back, and Danny picked up the shotgun by the barrel. As the boy rolled over and grabbed him by the legs, Danny lifted the shotgun, ready to strike.

A split second before he smashed the boy in the head, Danny froze.

He dropped the shotgun. He also dropped his jaw. The boy was not a boy. A teenage girl sat up, rubbing her skinned elbows.

"You didn't have to do that," she said. "I've never shot anybody."

Chapter 2
Shotguns and Scalping

"You said you were going to shoot me," Danny reminded her. "I'm sorry. I didn't mean to hurt you."

"You're not out of danger yet," the girl said. "My dad heard the shot. I know he did, and he's on his way here now. You better hide."

Danny took Fire Eye by the reins and hurried to a thick clump of trees. He knelt down behind a tree stump and pulled Fire Eye close. He watched as the girl reloaded her shotgun. She dipped a cup in the spring and took a long sip of water. Then she sat on the rocks, waiting for her father.

She could have killed me, thought Danny.

He never heard the footsteps of someone creeping up behind him. But he did hear the voice, four inches from his ear. It was a quiet voice, serious and strong.

"Make a move and you're a dead man," the voice said.

Danny froze.

"Lift your hands above your head. Now turn around, real slow."

Danny did as he was told. A tall, thin man faced him. He had a dark beard and green eyes.

He's the same age as my father, Danny thought. *Maybe forty years old.*

"Are you alone?" the man asked.

"Yes," Danny said.

"You're lying. How many are with you?"

"I am alone."

"Don't move," the man said. "Sarah!" he shouted. "Are you safe?"

"Yes, Dad," Sarah called out.

"Wait where you are, Sarah. We'll come to you," her dad said. He stuck the rifle barrel in Danny's back. "Take your horse by the reins and move. And don't forget, if you try to run, I'll shoot you."

Soon Danny and her father joined Sarah by the spring.

"What was he doing? Did he hurt you?" her father asked.

"No, Dad. I saw him getting a drink, the boy and his horse. I tried to shoot him, but I missed," Sarah said.

"Did you see any other Indians?"

"No. But if there are more Indians, they would have heard the shot," said Sarah. "They would be here by now."

"Unless they're hiding out, waiting till dark," her father said.

Sarah and her father looked to the hills surrounding them. After a long look, their eyes met. Danny saw fear on their faces, the fear of being attacked at night while they slept.

"If you *are* alone," asked Sarah's father, "what are you doing? Make me believe you, if you want to live."

Danny took a long breath. "I am going to my family," he said. "I was a prisoner at Fort Davis. I am going to my family."

"Why were you a prisoner?" he asked. "What did you do?"

"I am Navajo. That is all I did," said Danny. "The soldiers burned our homes. They killed our sheep. We did nothing."

Danny slowly turned his face away. The memories returned. He remembered Crowfoot, his favorite sheep. The soldiers cut the throats of the sheep. They made Danny watch as his sheep bled to death.

Danny had tried to save Crowfoot. He had grabbed him and run away. But a soldier shot Crowfoot, shot him in the head. Crowfoot died in Danny's arms, covering them both in blood.

"Look at me, boy!" Sarah's father shouted. He grabbed Danny's face and whipped it around.

Danny eyes were filled with tears. For the first time since he left his family, he shook with sobs. His chest heaved, and he cried aloud. He wrapped his arms around his chest, embarrassed that they would see him cry.

"I want to see my family," he finally said. "I am alone."

"Dad," said Sarah. "Don't be mean to him. He's telling us the truth, can't you see?"

Sarah's father lowered his shotgun. He reached his hand to Danny. Danny had seen enough white men to understand a handshake. He lifted his hand.

"My name is Bill Grady," Sarah's father said.

"My name is Danny Blackgoat," said Danny. "Nice to meet you."

Bill Grady smiled. "My wife has lunch ready. Would you like to eat with us?"

"Yes," Danny said. "I am hungry. I would like to eat with you."

"I'll run and tell Mom," Sarah said, dashing away.

"She doesn't have any friends," Mr. Grady said. "She'll want to know everything about you."

Bill Grady knew his daughter well. She and her mother served a lunch of beef stew and corn bread. The stew was thick and delicious.

Better than anything at the fort, Danny thought.

Mrs. Grady was at least a foot shorter than her husband. She was thin, too. She had a friendly face, reddish hair, and green eyes.

"Take all you want," she said to Danny.

Danny never looked up. He was shy, even around Navajo friends. And now he sat at a table in the home of white people.

"Danny Blackgoat," Sarah said. "I like your name. It's different, but I like it."

She waited for Danny to reply. He looked at his stew and said nothing.

"What's it like to be an Indian?" Sarah asked. Without waiting for an answer, she continued. "I bet you do war dances and scalp people. Did you ever scalp anybody?"

"I don't think so," Danny said. "What is *scalp*?"

"Sarah," Mrs. Grady said, "let Danny eat."

"I just want to know," said Sarah. She turned to Danny and said, "Scalp is when you cut somebody's hair off."

"My grandmother does that," said Danny.

"Your grandmother!" Sarah yelled. "Your grandmother *scalps* people?"

"Yes," said Danny. "But only when they need it."

"What?" shouted Sarah. "Mother, did you hear what he said? His grandmother *scalps* people!"

The Gradys laughed, a big hearty laugh, but not Sarah.

"What's funny about that?"

"Did I do something wrong?" Danny asked. He lowered his eyes and stared at his plate.

"No, Danny," said Mr. Grady. "You did nothing wrong."

"Then why is everybody laughing at me?"

"I'm not laughing at you," yelled Sarah. "I want to hit you! Where is my shotgun?"

"Sarah, sit down," said Mr. Grady, rocking back and forth in laughter as he said it.

"I am not eating at the table with this boy who thinks it's all right if his grandmother scalps people!" said Sarah, all in one long breath. She plopped into her seat and crossed her arms. "You can't make me eat," she whispered.

"Sarah, Danny's grandmother cuts people's hair," said Mrs. Grady. "Like I cut yours, but only when you need it, just like his grandmother does."

"That's not what he said," said Sarah.

"He doesn't know what *scalp* means," said her mother.

While Sarah and her mother spoke, Mr. Grady looked at Danny, alone and afraid.

"Danny," he said. "Nobody is mad at you. We don't always know what somebody is saying."

"Scalping is bad, isn't it?" asked Danny.

"Yes," said Mr. Grady. "*Scalping* is when someone kills another person and takes his hair—like a trophy."

"No Navajo would do that," said Danny. "I have heard of it, but none of my people would ever do that."

"Let us hope we never meet anyone who would," said Mr. Grady.

Soon Danny Blackgoat and the Gradys, his new friends, finished their noon meal.

"I need to go," Danny said. "Thank you. The food was good."

Sarah and her father packed a saddlebag with hard bread and cooked beef for Danny. The Gradys stood as Danny mounted Fire Eye and patted her neck.

"Good-bye," he said, lifting his hand to wave. He tugged the reins and urged Fire Eye up the hill and in the direction of the road.

The Gradys stood watching long after Danny had disappeared over the hill.

"I am afraid for him," said Mr. Grady.

"That talk of scalping seemed funny at the time," said Mrs. Grady. "But I don't like to think of it."

Sarah said what they were all thinking.

"Please don't let the scalping ones find him. Or us."

Chapter 3
Danger in the Shadows

Rick should be here soon, Danny thought. He looked up and down the road. There was no one on the road as far as Danny could see.

From the time of his escape, the plan was to meet Rick, who drove a supply wagon. Rick was a white man who was married to a Navajo woman. He was a good friend and would do anything to help Danny Blackgoat.

I can't be careless, Danny thought. *Not again. Sarah almost shot me this morning. I should stay out of sight until Rick shows up.*

He turned Fire Eye, and they moved into a clump of scrub oak trees. He steered his horse through broken branches and thin tree trunks. He stopped when he felt he couldn't be seen from the road.

"This should be safe, boy," he said, patting Fire Eye on the neck.

He eased himself from the saddle and tied Fire Eye to a tree trunk. Now that he was settled, Danny worried about his friend. Rick was driving a wagon of food supplies through dangerous territory.

Danny's father had talked of raiders who burned homes and took children to sell as slaves. But they stayed away from Navajo communities, like Danny's home at Canyon de Chelly.

"We look out for each other," his father had said. "The slave traders look for travelers or people living away from others. They're easier to capture."

"Sarah and her family don't know how much their lives are in danger. Every day," Danny whispered.

He saw the dust rising on the road long before he saw his friend. In less than an hour Rick appeared, driving his wagon on the road below. Danny climbed on Fire Eye's back and tugged the reins.

"Easy, Fire Eye," he said, as he led his horse down the hill and onto the road.

"Whoa!" Rick shouted, pulling his mules to a halt. "Danny Blackgoat, I never thought I'd see the day." Rick leaped from his wagon, and Danny stepped down from Fire Eye to meet him.

"What's it like," Rick asked, "spending the day in a coffin?"

"I don't want to do it again," said Danny.

"Tell me what happened," Rick said.

"Do you really want to hear this?" Danny asked.

"Yes, I do," said Rick. "Jim Davis couldn't tell me much. He was being very careful."

For the next half hour Danny told Rick about his last days at Fort Davis, a Texas prison fort.

"As you know," Danny began, "Jim Davis came up with a plan to help me escape. He was the carpenter, so he built the coffins when somebody died. The bodies were buried outside the gates of the fort. The plan was for him to build the coffin deeper than usual. I would sneak out of the barracks and climb inside the coffin. The next day, during the funeral, I'd be buried with the body. Then Davis would find a horse for me and dig me up the next morning. I'd be free!"

Rick nodded, his eyes growing wide as he listened to the story.

"Everything went like we planned," Danny said. "But I didn't look at the other body in the coffin when I crawled in. I was too scared. That morning, the soldiers dragged the coffin to the graveyard, outside of the fort, and buried us both—me and the dead person. It was the longest day of my life. I thought of my family. I thought of my friends. I knew if I died they would never find my body. Did Jim Davis tell you what he did?"

"He only said they would bury you and that you would escape from the graveyard. That's all he told me," Rick said.

"Well, they did bury me. But before they did, Jim Davis laid his leather vest on the body, so I wouldn't be afraid. But I had my eyes closed when I climbed into the coffin. When I felt the vest, I thought Jim Davis was dead and that he was buried with me. I thought I'd never get out of the coffin alive!"

Rick laughed and laughed. "I'm sorry, Danny," he said. "But now that you're alive, it does make for a good story!"

Danny smiled. "Yes, I'm alive," he said. "And he brought me Fire Eye, the best horse in the world."

Rick gripped him by the shoulders. "Danny, I was so afraid for you. We all were. My wife and daughter Jane send their best wishes."

"Tell them I will miss them," Danny said. "I will see them again. I don't know when, but I will."

"Oh, I almost forgot," Rick said. "Jim Davis wanted me to give you this. He said it might save your life."

Rick lifted a leather pouch from his wagon and handed Danny a knife. The blade was five inches long with a sharp point.

"It's called a bowie knife," Rick said. "No one knew he had it."

Danny's eyes grew big. He had never seen a knife like this before.

"A gift for me?"

"Yes," Rick said. "And Davis said to remind you that he wants a letter someday. When you learn to write."

"Tell him I will learn to write. For him."

"I will," Rick said. "Now, we should be going. I think it's safer if you ride with me. I carry prisoners all the time. No one will think it's unusual."

"What about Fire Eye?" Danny asked.

"We can tie him to the wagon. He'll be fine."

For the remainder of the day, Danny rode beside Rick. As the sky darkened, they neared a watering hole.

"You should climb in the back," Rick said. "Everybody waters their animals here. No reason to take any chances."

Danny climbed into the back of the wagon and settled on the wooden floor.

Rick always watered his mules by daylight, but had waited for Danny to get a good head start from Fort Davis. Now he pulled into the watering hole several hours later than usual.

A band of slave traders heard the wagon approaching. They didn't speak a word. They silently hid in the shadows and watched. When they saw a white man watering his mules, they relaxed.

As slave traders, they sold people, but this white man was too old for anyone to want him. They could steal his horse. There were six of them. It would be easy. They could take his mules and leave him on foot.

"Danny," Rick shouted. "Are you awake?"

Who is he talking to? the slave traders thought. They froze and waited. Suddenly, a new voice caught their attention.

"Is it safe?" Danny asked.

"If anybody's here, I don't see 'em," Rick replied.

Danny climbed from the rear of the wagon.

When the slave traders saw Danny, they knew what to do. Young men sold well in the slave market. Moving quietly, they climbed on their horses. They were not afraid of Danny. The man would be armed, but not the Navajo boy.

The six men soon surrounded Rick's wagon. While Danny and Rick knelt down by the water, one man rode behind the wagon. He untied the horse. Fire Eye snorted and stomped the ground.

"Sounds like he's ready to drink," Rick said.

He never said another word. A stranger stepped from behind a tree and struck him in the head with a stone club. Rick fell to the ground and lay without moving. Blood flowed from a cut above his broken nose.

Chapter 4
A Bargain with Death

Two men knelt below the bed of the wagon. When Danny stepped to the ground, they grabbed him from behind. One man put a sack over his head and tied it tightly around his neck. The other tied his hands behind his back.

Unable to see, Danny kicked out at his captors. He heard their laughter.

"Who are you kicking, boy?" one man asked. He picked up a handful of dirt and tossed it at Danny.

Danny shook his head in anger. A man took him by the shoulders and spun him around and around. Danny grew more and more dizzy, until he finally fell to the ground.

"Let him lay there," a man said. "We need to finish off the old man."

They mean Rick, Danny thought. *They are going to kill him!*

"Manny, you want me to shoot him?" one man asked.

"No, Marcos," Manny replied. "A gun makes too much noise. Finish him with the club. Then toss his body over the hill. After the buzzards are done with him, nobody will know what happened."

Danny feared for his friend's life. *I have to stop them,* he thought. *Rick was only here to help me. I can't let them kill him.*

"Wait!" Danny shouted.

"You better shut up!" said Manny. "You're lucky to be alive."

"Just listen to me," Danny said. "I can lead you to a ranch. Many workers live there. Not far from here."

"Why would you do that?" Manny asked.

"I want you to let the old man live," Danny said. "He didn't see any of you. Just leave him here."

"Even if we let him live," said Manny, "you're coming with us."

"I will," said Danny. "I won't be any trouble. I will take you to the ranch."

So far, the men had spoken English. Danny could understand everything they said. But now they spoke another language, one he didn't understand.

"Que piensas, Manny?" asked Marcos. "What do you think?"

"Si habla la verdad, es bueno. Mas jovenes, mas dinero," Manny said. "If he speaks the truth, it's good. More young men, more money."

Danny guessed what they were saying.

"I am telling the truth," he said. "Many good workers and few guns. They won't have any guards at night."

"You're a smart young man," said Manny. "Smart enough to know what happens if you are lying."

"I am not lying," Danny said. "Let's go now. We can get there while it's still dark. They'll be asleep."

"Take the sack from his head," Manny said. "But keep his hands tied."

Danny kept his eyes to the ground. When the sack was removed, he took a deep breath. He could at least see the slave traders.

The six men surrounding him were a mixed band of Mexican and white people. *But no Navajos,* Danny thought.

The one thing they all had in common was a meanness in their eyes. *They would do whatever Manny says. They would kill Rick— or me—as easily as they would slap a fly,* he thought.

"You ride with me," Manny said. "On the saddle behind me. Take us to this ranch." Two men lifted Danny onto Manny's horse.

"What about the old man?" asked Marcos.

"Tie him up and leave him," Manny said. "If this boy is lying, we'll be back." He turned to Danny, saying, "Which way to this ranch?

"Down the hill and east," Danny said, pointing.

"Put your hands on my shoulder," Manny said. "And don't move them unless you ask my permission. You understand me?"

"Yes," Danny said, lifting his bound wrists to Manny's right shoulder.

Now, Danny thought, *I wait and I watch. The time will come when they will let their guard down. I must be ready.*

Danny still had his bowie knife, his gift from Jim Davis. It was tied to his ankle, under his pants leg. And he had the beginning of a plan.

"How far to the ranch?" Manny asked.

"A three-hour ride," Danny said. "There is a watering hole there, too."

"How come we don't know about this watering hole?" asked Manny. "I'm warning you, boy. If you want to live, don't lie to me."

"I am not lying to you," said Danny.

The slave traders eased their horses down the hill. Moving from the trees to the road, they entered the light of a full moon.

We will arrive at the ranch before sunrise, Danny thought. *I hope I am still alive to say the morning prayer and greet the dawn.* He wanted to touch the leather pouch hanging around his neck, filled with corn pollen. *It was a gift from Rick's wife*, he remembered. *I hope Rick is safe.*

While his mules slept nearby, Rick lay in a pool of his own blood. His hands were tied, and he was barely breathing.

Chapter 5
Fire Eye's Bloody Saddle

As the moon crept over the sky, the slave traders rode east, in the direction of the Grady ranch. They rode in the middle of the road, in full view.

They are not afraid of anybody, Danny thought. *That's good. They will never suspect what they are riding into.*

The hours dragged on and the men grew sleepy. Pretending to fall asleep, Danny let his hands slip from Manny's shoulder.

"Hey, boy!" Manny shouted.

"I'm sorry," Danny said, shaking his head back and forth. "I fell asleep."

Half an hour later, he let his hands slide down again. He leaned his head against Manny's back. Danny waited for Manny to holler at him again, but he didn't.

He thinks I have fallen asleep, Danny thought. Very slowly, he slid his hand to his ankle. He lifted his knife and tucked it into his belt. His knife was still unseen, but would be easy to grab when he needed it.

Several times he jerked himself, as if he were waking up suddenly.

"I'm sorry," he said, sputtering his words. "I'm sorry. Was I sleeping?"

"Try to stay awake," Manny said. "How far to the ranch?"

Danny lifted himself on the saddle and looked down the road. "Not far now," he said. "Maybe an hour."

Manny rode for another hour. Then he pulled his horse to a stop.

"*Arrete,*" he shouted. "Stop!"

The men surrounded him, waiting for orders.

"Boy," he said, turning to Danny. "Start talking. Tell us about the ranch."

"When we come to the trees," Danny said, "ride over the hill. The watering hole is on the other side. There is a clump of trees around the spring. The ranch house is half a mile away, hidden by the trees. No one will see us. You can attack the ranch house from the trees."

"Good," said Manny. "And I do not need to warn you what will happen if you are lying to us."

"I understand," said Danny.

"*Escuche,*" Manny said. "Listen! We will have a new leader today. Bring the boy's horse. He will lead us down the hill. If he's lying, they will shoot him first."

He turned to Danny. "If you try to get away, we'll have our guns at your back. You'll never make it. Both you and your friend will die."

Danny said nothing. He kept his eyes to the ground to hide his excitement. His plan was still brewing. But he knew he had a chance with Fire Eye.

I have my knife and my horse, he thought. *Both gifts from Jim Davis.*

"Lead us to the watering hole," Manny said. "Boy, you say we can see the ranch house from the trees?"

"Yes," Danny replied.

"Good," Manny said. "Men, we'll stay together in the trees and plan our attack. Be careful and quiet. Keep your guns ready. If you have to shoot, do not shoot to kill. Remember, the men and women at the ranch will be our slaves. We want them to bring a good price."

Danny's eyes grew big. *The men and women would be slaves?* he thought. *I never knew they were capturing women, too! Sarah. And her mother. I have brought danger to the Gradys. What am I doing?*

"What's keeping you, boy?" Manny said. "Get on your horse and take us there."

Danny climbed down from Manny's horse and mounted Fire Eye.

I know what I am doing, he thought. *I am trying to save the life of my friend, Rick. I hope I'm not bringing death on us all.*

The moon slipped behind the clouds, casting dark shadows on the hillside. Danny led Fire Eye up the slope, patting him on the neck.

"Good boy, Fire Eye," he whispered. "Danny is here. Go slow and easy."

Fire Eye shook his head and blew a soft breath of air.

He knows to be quiet, thought Danny. *Fire Eye is smart.*

As they topped the hill, the clouds parted. Moonlight shone on the spring water below. Danny reached for his knife. He knew the time was near. He had to make his move.

Instead, Fire Eye made it for him. He stepped on a thin sheet of rock. It crushed beneath his weight, and Fire Eye stumbled. Only for a brief moment, but it was enough. Danny rolled forward in the saddle. He gripped his knife to keep from dropping it, and the blade cut deep into his palm.

Blood gushed from Danny's hand, covering Fire Eye and the saddle.

If Fire Eye's bloody saddle doesn't warn them, nothing will! thought Danny.

He tumbled from the saddle to the ground. As he fell, he gently stuck the point of his knife in Fire Eye's hindquarters.

"Go, boy! Run!" he said in a loud whisper. "Find Sarah!"

Fire Eye sprang to life. He lifted his front legs from the ground and let fly with the loudest cry Danny had ever heard from a horse!

"Wheeeeeee!"

When his front legs struck the ground, Fire Eye took off running.

"Follow him!" shouted Manny. "He'll wake them up."

The men at the Grady ranch were already awake. They had spotted the slave traders as they topped the hill. Seeing Fire Eye running in their direction, they aimed their guns and waited.

The slave traders followed Fire Eye, riding at a slow and careful pace. Their guns were strapped to their saddles. They had expected an easy ride to the watering hole before they began their attack. As the slave traders rode down the hill, they were met with the guns of ten men and one strong young lady.

Danny had heard the blast of the shotgun that killed his favorite sheep, Crowfoot, and Crowfoot's blood had covered him. But Danny had never heard the sound of a dozen shotguns firing at the same time, again and again.

He crawled to the edge of the hill. Gunfire rocked the valley. With every shot, a puff of smoke rose from the dark trees.

"Look at them," Danny said to himself. "They must have known the slave traders were nearby. Mr. Grady and all of his men are here!"

Manny's men tried to halt their horses, but they had nowhere to go. The horses panicked. Rocks exploded around them. When the first horse was hit, he flopped on his side and slid down the hill, dragging his rider with him.

Chapter 6
Bodies on the Hillside

"Fire Eye," Sarah shouted, tossing her shotgun aside. "Here, boy!"

Fire Eye knew Sarah's voice. Even surrounded by the noise of the shotguns, he knew *that* voice. He crossed the spring and entered the dark woods.

"Over here!" Sarah shouted. As Fire Eye rubbed against her, Sarah felt the wetness of Danny's blood before she saw it. "Fire Eye, you splashed yourself," she said, covering her ears from the gunfire.

"Here, let me dry you off." Sarah lifted her sleeve and wiped his saddle. A soft breeze blew the tree branches, just enough to let the moon squeeze through. In the yellow light, Sarah saw the blood.

"No!" she cried out. "Where is Danny? What did they do to him?"

"Sarah," her father shouted. "We need you! Get your shotgun."

Sarah turned from Fire Eye. She lifted her gun and took careful aim. The fallen horse had stopped his slide. His rider, bruised and battered, tried to stand.

"This is for Danny Blackgoat," Sarah whispered. She pulled the trigger. The blast knocked her to the ground. When she stood up, she saw the rider. He fell on his back and grabbed his leg.

She had hit him just above the knee.

"Nice shot, Sarah," her father said. "I think that's the last of them."

Mr. Grady was wrong.

Only five men lay on the hillside. Manny stood by his horse on the hilltop, watching the bloodshed below. He cast one final look at his followers. One man rolled to his knees and tried to stand. He stumbled back and forth, then fell on his face. Another clutched his stomach. Their horses surrounded the slave traders. They flapped their tails and snorted, unsure of what to do.

But Manny knew what to do. As the only survivor of the attack, he turned his anger toward Danny. He climbed the hill and looked among the rocks and scrub bushes. For half an hour he searched. As the morning sun crept over the hills, he turned his horse to the road.

"You better stay hid, boy!" he shouted over his shoulder. "But know this. If it takes me the rest of my life, I will find you. First, I'm going for your friend! You lied to me, and he's a dead man."

As Manny fled, Mr. Grady led his men from the woods. They carried their shotguns in front of them, ready to fire. They moved slowly, silent and strong. At that moment the sun topped the hill, shining on the gun barrels. Danny gasped at the sight.

"They look like warriors," he whispered.

They walked from one wounded man to another, taking any weapons—pistols, shotguns, and knives—in belts or hidden in boots. All of the slave traders were wounded, but they were alive. They rolled away from Mr. Grady's men, covering their eyes. They expected to be killed. This was the way of the lawless life they lived.

"Stand guard over them, two men to every one," Mr. Grady said. "We can let the soldiers know we've caught them. Those who live will end up at the Fort Davis prison camp."

"I'll bring bandages," said a young man. "We can try to stop the bleeding till a doctor comes." He climbed on his horse and rode to the barn.

"Sarah," Mr. Grady shouted. "Better let your mother know we're safe. Tell her we'll be ready for breakfast. Let her know that nobody's hurt. None of us are, at least."

"Yes, Dad," Sarah said. "I'll let her know." As she dashed through the woods, Sarah spotted Fire Eye. She saw the streaks of red covering his neck and shoulders.

"Danny's blood," she said. "I don't ever want to wash that blood away." She mounted Fire Eye and took the reins in both hands.

"Let's go, boy," she said, and Fire Eye leaped at her command. Sarah snapped the reins and Fire Eye streaked from the woods. As she neared the ranch house, Sarah called out.

"Mom!" she shouted. "We're all safe. Nobody's hurt!"

Mrs. Grady stepped to the porch. She held her hand to her forehead, looking very nervous.

"Is your father safe?" Mrs. Grady asked. Her voice cracked as she spoke.

"Yes," said Sarah, "everybody is. We caught five bad men. I shot one."

"Oh, Sarah. You didn't need to shoot anybody."

"Yes, Mom, I did," said Sarah. She stepped from Fire Eye and tied his reins to a post. "Mom, Danny Blackgoat is dead."

"That poor boy! What happened?"

"We don't know for sure. But look," Sarah said, pointing to Fire Eye's saddle. "That is Danny's blood. I know it is."

"Where is Danny's body?" Mrs. Grady asked.

"I don't know," Sarah said. "The bad men must have killed him last night."

"Where is your father?" Mrs. Grady asked.

"Taking care of the prisoners," said Sarah. "Bandaging their wounds. Dad and the men are coming for breakfast soon."

"Well," Mrs. Grady said, "let's cook enough for everybody."

"Mom, can we say a special prayer at breakfast? For Danny Blackgoat?" Sarah asked. She hung her head and wiped tears from her eyes. Mrs. Grady held her daughter close.

"We will do something special for Danny," Mrs. Grady said. "Now, let's get breakfast started."

An hour later, Mr. Grady led the wounded slave traders to the barn. "You two stand guard," he said, nodding to his most dependable workers. "We'll save some breakfast for you."

Meals at the Gradys' were served on a long wooden table on the back porch. Sarah and Mrs. Grady covered the table with pots of potatoes and pans of fried eggs. The outside air was chilly. Small clouds of mist rose from the steaming food.

Mr. Grady sat at the head of the table, surrounded by his men. When everyone was seated, they waited in silence. Mr. Grady began every meal with a prayer of thanks.

Today was unlike any day they had known. They felt like celebrating their victory. But the sound of the shotguns still rang in their ears. The sight of blood flowing down the hill wouldn't go away. This was a morning to be thankful, but not to celebrate.

Mrs. Grady had placed four candles from one end of the table to the other.

"The candles are for Christmas," she announced. "It's only seven days away."

The men nodded without speaking. Sarah sat next to her father. She leaned against him and whispered, "Dad, please pray for Danny Blackgoat."

Mr. Grady nodded without opening his eyes. He put a finger to his lips.

People always want me to be quiet, Sarah thought.

Mr. Grady stood. "Dear Lord," he began, "we have much to be thankful for today. We thank you for our lives. You saw us through danger. We are still safe and together."

He paused and the men offered quiet *ums* and *amens*.

"We want to remember a young friend today," Mr. Grady said. He lowered his voice to almost a whisper. "He came into our lives for only a short time."

As Mr. Grady began his prayer, Danny crossed the field and approached the house. He saw everyone seated at the table. Their heads were bowed and their eyes were closed. Not wanting to disturb anyone, Danny sat at one end of a long bench. He was so quiet, not even Mr. Grady heard him.

"He was loved by us," Mr. Grady continued, his eyes still closed. "We will miss him."

Who is he talking about? wondered Danny.

"We have only his horse to remember him by," said Mr. Grady. "Please help Sarah. She will care for his horse, Lord, and you will care for us all."

Danny leaned over to the man sitting next to him. He cupped his hand beside his mouth and whispered, "What horse?"

"Fire Eye," the man said, keeping his eyes closed. "Danny Blackgoat's horse."

"What if Danny wants his horse back?" Danny asked.

"Danny has no use for his horse."

"Why not?"

"Danny Blackgoat is dead."

"I am not dead!" Danny shouted. Everyone opened their eyes and turned to look at him. Mr. Grady dropped his jaw.

"Sorry," said Danny. Everyone was staring at him!

"Dannnnnnn-eeeeeeeee!" Sarah hollered from the far end of the table. "I knew you would return! Dad, look, Danny Blackgoat has crawled out of the grave!"

"Yes, I did," said Danny, shrugging his shoulders. "But that was yesterday. And how did you know about that?"

Chapter 7
Manny Seeks Revenge

Manny urged his horse into a gallop. He rode for an hour at top speed, until his horse breathed hard and slowed to a walk. Manny spotted a group of twisted mesquite trees by the roadside. He pulled his horse to a halt. He saw a trickle of water bubbling from the rocks and stepped to the ground.

"*Ay,*" he whispered, patting his horse on the neck, "*agua para mi caballo.*" He took the reins and led his horse to the spring. Manny sat and watched while his horse drank big gulps of water. His horse panted and heaved, weary from the long ride at top speed.

I will kill the old man, Manny thought. *And someday I will find that Indian boy. I'll punish him, bad, and then sell him to the meanest slave master I can find. He'll spend the rest of his life being sorry he lied to me.*

When his horse was rested, Manny mounted him and led him in a slow trot, closer and closer to Rick.

When Rick woke up, he was lying face down in a pool of dried blood. He rolled to his back and looked up at the afternoon sky. His head throbbed in pain from his broken nose. Dried blood covered his lips and cheeks. He reached to touch his nose.

"Yow!" he hollered. When he realized his nose was broken, Rick stood up slowly and looked for his wagon. He spotted it, standing where he and Danny had planned to settle in for the night.

"Where is that boy?" Rick whispered to himself. "I hope he's safe."

Rick saw his mules still hitched to the wagon.

"Danny!" he called out.

When Danny didn't answer, Rick pieced together what had happened. He saw the footprints of several men and tracks of their horses surrounding the wagon.

That looks like Danny's footprints, he thought, staring at the ground behind the wagon. He saw the stirred-up dirt where the men had captured Danny.

"Looks like he put up a fight," Rick said aloud. "I hope he's smart enough to let them have their way, at least for a while."

Rick closed his eyes and smiled. "Yes," he said, as if talking to Danny, "you're that smart. You wouldn't be alive, with all you've gone through, if you weren't."

Rick followed the horse tracks to the top of the hill.

I wonder why they left me alive? he asked himself. *I wonder if Danny had anything to do with that?*

Rick looked up and down the road until he spotted a rising cloud of dust and a rider coming from the east. *If I can make it down the hill in time, he can help me*, he thought.

Rick waved his arms and called out, but the rider never heard him. Soon, the rider turned his horse uphill. *Why would he be coming this way?* Rick asked himself. *He acts like he knows where he's going.*

Rick jumped behind a boulder just as Manny rode past him. The mean look on Manny's face and the roll of shotgun shells across his chest told Rick everything he needed to know about this strange rider.

"He's headed to my wagon," Rick said in a whisper. "He knows where Danny Blackgoat is!"

Rick knew that his life, and the life of Danny Blackgoat, depended on what he did next. He crouched behind the boulder and wrapped his arms around himself in a blanket of thought.

I'm an older fellow, not young and quick like he is, he thought. *So I have to take him by surprise. And he has the guns. They took mine.*

Rick looked at the ground and the scrub trees surrounding the boulder. He smiled at his own thinking. *If I lived in a time before guns, what would I use as a weapon?*

The plants and rocks around him seemed to glow in answer to his question.

Yes, I see you, he nodded to a pile of stones. Some were round and some were thin and sharp. He looked above him and saw a thick tree branch, cracked and almost touching the ground. Very quietly he stood. He saw the back of Manny, riding to the wagon.

He's going there to finish me off, he thought. *I'll do my best to make sure that doesn't happen!*

Rick twisted the branch and broke it off the tree limb. With the sharp stone, he carved a long, thin point on the end of the branch. *I've never used a sword in battle, but it won't hurt to have it handy.*

Next, he took off his shirt and tied it around his waist, making a deep pocket for carrying stones. He gathered a dozen stones the size of his fist, and one large, flat stone.

Now for a club, he thought. At that very moment, his nose began to throb in pain. *I think I know what broke my nose!*

He tore a strip of cloth from his shirt and picked a stone from his pocket. He tied the stone to a short, thick branch. With his pocket full of stones for throwing, his sword in his belt, and his club in his hand, Rick took a deep breath and prepared his mind for the battle to come.

"I'm as ready as I'll ever be," he said to himself. Rick knelt to the ground, whispered a quiet prayer, and stepped from behind the boulder. Staying in the shadows of the trees, he ran in a low crouch to his wagon.

I'd better not follow the same path as before, he thought. *By now he's found the spot where they left me. He knows I'm gone, and he'll follow my footprints.*

Rick circled through the trees and approached his wagon from the other side. He heard Manny before he saw him.

"You better run, old man," Manny shouted. "When I catch you, I'll tie you to the ground and the desert will eat you alive!"

Rick flung himself to the ground before he realized that Manny hadn't actually seen him.

Manny was just talking out loud to himself in anger. Rick shivered to think of what Manny would do to him if he found him. He had seen horses die in the hot desert. He had seen how the ants crawled over them. He had watched the small animals gnaw on their bones, and saw how the buzzards fought over the meat.

"That will not happen to me or Danny," he whispered. "Not today. Not ever."

Rick knew he had the element of surprise in his favor. Manny expected him to run. *He would never expect me to come after him,* Rick thought. *Now, where is the last place he would expect me to be?*

With a big grin, Rick realized he was staring at the answer to his question. *My wagon!*

While Manny searched the trees and bushes for him, Rick crawled quietly to the rear of the wagon. He lifted himself from the ground and hid in the shadows of the covered wagon bed.

Now for the hardest part, he told himself. *The waiting.*

He did not have long to wait. Manny saw Rick's footprints in the dry dirt. He followed them to the rear of the wagon. He stopped his horse ten feet from the wagon. Rick lifted the club and aimed it at the back of Manny's head. *Move just a little closer*, Rick thought, *and you're mine*.

Suddenly, Manny turned away from the wagon. Rick followed his gaze. He saw a cloud of dust and a horse and rider hurrying down the hill.

"Rick!" a voice called out. It was the voice of Danny Blackgoat.

A mean grin crept across Manny's face. "I couldn't ask for more than this," he said.

Manny lifted his shotgun and waited for Danny to enter the clearing.

Chapter 8
Food for the Desert?

"Slow down, Fire Eye," Danny said, patting his horse on the neck. "We're here now. Rick will be glad to see us."

Rick was not glad to see him, but Manny was. He took careful aim at the dust cloud moving in and out of the trees, knowing that soon Danny would come into view.

Rick slowly rose and lifted the club over his head. *If I miss, Danny and I are both dead.*

He saw Manny squint his eyes and lean his head on the barrel of the shotgun.

"He's about to fire," Rick whispered. "It's now or never."

"Danny Blackgoat!" he shouted as a warning, before he leaped from the back of the wagon. With all of his leg strength, Rick pushed himself from the wagon. He swung the club as he jumped.

Manny jerked his head around just in time to catch the stone club on the side of his head. His horse reared and bolted, throwing Manny to the ground. His shotgun flew from his grasp.

Rick landed hard but quickly scrambled to his feet. He grabbed his wooden sword and stuck the point in Manny's neck. Manny lay face down.

"I've got a gun pointed at the back of your head," Rick said, hoping Manny would believe his lie. "You tried to kill me," Rick said. "And you almost shot my friend. If you want to live, don't move."

Soon Danny rode into the clearing and pulled Fire Eye to a halt. He saw Rick, still bloody from his broken nose, standing over Manny with only a wooden sword. He knew better than to talk. He quickly grabbed Manny's rifle and moved beside Rick.

"Now you have your own shotgun pointed at your head, by a young man who'd be glad to use it," said Rick. Turning to Danny, he said, "Keep the gun on him. If he moves, shoot him."

Rick gathered rope from his wagon and tied Manny's hands behind his back.

"Now get up and walk to the tree in front of you," he said. "Slow, real slow." Manny struggled to his feet. He turned his head and faced Rick and Danny.

"Just get this over with," he said with a sneer. "Shoot me and be on your way. Because if I ever get out of this alive, I think you know what will happen. I will never rest till both of you are dead."

"Do what I say if you want to live," said Rick. "Lean up against the tree and stay still."

Rick tied Manny's legs to the trunk of the tree. He wrapped the rope several times around the tree and Manny. When he finished, he turned to Danny. "He's not going anywhere now," he said.

"We should do one more thing," Danny said. "Something Manny taught me."

He climbed in the wagon and returned with a small bag.

"Here," he said to Rick. "Put this over his face. If he hears someone coming, he won't know whether to shout or be silent. He won't know who it is. That's what they did to me."

"You are a quick learner, son," said Rick.

"I've learned things I wish I didn't know," Danny said.

"Tell me what happened, Danny. The last thing I remember, you were in the back of the wagon. We had just pulled into this clearing."

Danny glanced at Manny and nodded to a clump of trees a short distance away.

"You don't want him to hear," Rick said, pointing to Manny.

"Yes," Danny said, as they walked to the trees and settled on a log.

For the next quarter hour Danny told the story of everything he remembered. When he learned that Danny had made a bargain with the slave traders, a bargain that saved his life, Rick smiled.

"I owe you my life, Danny Blackgoat."

"And I owe you for mine, Rick," Danny said.

"Now," Rick said, "you have a choice to make."

"What choice?" Danny asked.

"What do we do with this man?" he said, pointing to Manny. "If we let him live, you know we'll never be safe. He'll hunt us both down."

"The soldiers are already looking for me," said Danny.

"Yes," said Rick, "but they won't kill you if they find you."

Danny waited for several minutes before answering.

"You don't know what they will do, Rick," he finally said. "They killed an old Navajo man, our friend and neighbor from home. He was a good man."

"Why?" asked Rick. "What did he do?"

"He walked too slowly," said Danny. "And when his daughter ran to help him, they shot her, too."

"I am sorry, Danny." He hung his head in sadness and shame. "At least your family is still alive. But before we see them, you have to decide what to do with this man. You have his shotgun, Danny. No one would blame you if you shot him."

"I am free to go. He is tied to a tree," said Danny. "I cannot kill him."

"No one would blame you, Danny," Rick said. "This man is a killer. He came back to kill me."

"But he cannot hurt us now," said Danny. "I am sorry, Rick. I can't shoot him."

"I thought you would say that, Danny. I'm not the killing kind either. Now, let's see if these horses can pull a wagon."

Soon Danny and Rick were steering the wagon uphill. As they left the clearing, Rick called over his shoulder to Manny, "We'll send someone back for you, as soon as I get to the fort. They'll know what to do with you."

As they eased the wagon onto the road, Rick said, "That stopover lasted a little longer than we expected."

Danny nodded, remembering the Grady family. "I hope my friends on the ranch will be safe," he said. "I hope I didn't bring trouble to them."

"These days," said Rick, "there's trouble every which way you turn."

Rick and Danny rode in silence for a long hour, lost in the world of their own thoughts. Danny wondered how his family was doing. Rick felt better than ever about the young man who sat beside him. Danny Blackgoat had passed a very important test.

Rick knew of the feelings between Danny and his daughter, Jane. In choosing not to kill Manny, Danny earned a new level of respect from Rick. *He is a man I would be proud to have in my family,* thought Rick.

Chapter 9
New Morning and an Old Voice

That afternoon they neared the road that led to Canyon de Chelly, Danny's home before he and his family were captured.

"I guess we'll soon be saying good-bye," Rick said.

"What do you mean?" asked Danny.

"We're almost to the north road," said Rick. "Turn north and you'll be home in a few days. This trouble will be behind you."

"I'm not going home," Danny said. "I could never leave my family. They are prisoners at Fort Sumner."

"What do you plan to do? As soon as the soldiers see you, they'll send you back to Fort Davis. And I wouldn't want to go there if I were you. You stole a horse, Danny. They hang men for stealing horses."

"I guess I'll have stay away from the soldiers," Danny said.

"You know you are risking your life?" asked Rick.

"I have to see my family," Danny said. "That was why I climbed in the coffin, so I could see my family. That was my gift from Jim Davis, to see my family."

They passed the north road in silence. Rick glanced over at Danny, who kept his eyes on the road in front of them.

"How far to the fort?" Danny asked.

"We could be there before sunset," Rick said. "But for your sake, Danny, I'll take it slow and easy. We'll arrive after dark."

"Thank you," Danny said. He still didn't know what he would do once they arrived at Fort Sumner.

Danny sat next to Rick as they rode, staring at the sandy land surrounding them. The trees were small and scrubby, what few there were.

"Mostly cactus," Danny said, almost talking to himself.

"Yes," Rick agreed. "Not much will grow in this dry land."

"Is there water at Fort Sumner, where my family is?" Danny asked.

Rick paused for a long time before replying. They came upon a skinny tree covered with gray leaves. He snapped the reins and led the horses and wagon under the tree.

"Time we take a break," he said. "Let these horses stand in the shade for a while. I could use a break myself." He stepped from the wagon and took the water bag from under the seat. "Let's get a drink, Danny."

"You always answer when I ask you something," Danny said. "What are you not telling me?"

Rick looked at him and smiled. "You are a smart one, Danny Blackgoat. You are right. I was avoiding telling you the truth about the water at Fort Sumner."

"The water is bad, isn't it?" Danny asked.

"Yes, Danny. The water is very bad," said Rick. "Navajo people are getting sick from the water. It is full of rocks and limestone.

Most of the soldiers drink water they bring from somewhere else. But there isn't enough water for the prisoners, the Navajos."

"Is my family sick?" Danny asked.

"I was carrying supplies to Fort Sumner two weeks ago, Danny. I looked in on your family, like I always try to do. Your sister had a fever. She had been on her back for four days, your mother said."

"I knew something bad would happen to my family," Danny said.

"They should never have built a fort in this desert," Rick said. "The commander lied about the water."

"We have to get there soon," Danny said, rising to his feet.

"Hold on, Danny. If you want to do your family any good, you can't be seen, remember," Rick said.

"I know, but I have to help them."

"All right," said Rick, "let's get moving. It will be after dark when we get there."

As they came closer to the fort, they were surrounded by tall hills covered with boulders, but there were few trees. They passed deep canyons of sandstone. Danny looked for any sign of water in the canyons. He saw none. *Rick was right*, he thought. *No one could live here without water.*

The sun floated like a big fireball, ducking only briefly behind a mesa, until they rode in the darkness.

"We have to find a place for you to hide, Danny," Rick said.

"I saw a canyon back there," Danny said, pointing over his shoulder. "I can stay there till you come for me."

"That's a good plan, Danny," Rick said. "Here, you take the water bag. I can get good water at the fort. Take some dried beef, too. I'll find a place to keep Fire Eye. He'll be there when you need him."

"Will you see my family tonight?" Danny asked.

"Yes, and I'll come to see you early in the morning. But be very careful, Danny. Make sure it's me and make sure I am alone."

"I will. Thank you, Rick," Danny said. He stepped from the wagon, carrying his supper of water and beef strips.

"You're welcome, Danny."

Danny hurried down the road to the canyon. He broke a thick branch from a tree and climbed down the steep wall. A thin slice of moon lit his way, from one sliding rock to another. He came upon a flat rock hanging over the canyon, making a small cave.

"This should be a good place to spend the night," he whispered to himself. "But I bet I'm not the only one to think that." He poked his stick into the cave, stirring up the dust.

"WHIRRRRR," came the reply.

A rattlesnake den, he thought. Danny slowly backed away from the cave. *Maybe it won't be so bad to sleep out in the open tonight.*

He found a big boulder and circled it, scratching the ground with his stick to make sure no rattlesnakes were nesting outside the den. When he confirmed that all was safe, he leaned against the boulder and enjoyed a long drink of fresh water.

As he chewed the beef strips, he said to himself, "My family will have good water. I will bring it to them."

The next morning, Danny woke up two hours before sunrise, as he did every morning. He climbed to the top of the boulder and waited. When the first rays of sunlight greeted him, he pulled corn pollen from his pouch and said the prayer his grandfather had taught him.

When morning casts its light on the canyon wall
A new house is made,
A house made of dawn.
Before me, everything is beautiful
Behind me, everything is beautiful
Above me, everything is beautiful
Below me, everything is beautiful
Around me, everything is beautiful
Within me, everything is beautiful.
Taja ahotahe, nothing will change.

As he climbed down from the boulder, Danny heard a horse on the road. He leaped behind the boulder and knelt in the shadow. Someone was sliding down the canyon. Soon they stood on the other side of the boulder. Danny heard whoever it was climbing the boulder.

They will see me, he thought. He stood to run, when he heard his name called.

"Danny. Danny Blackgoat."

The voice was not Rick's.

Chapter 10
The Family Blackgoat

Danny froze. He closed his eyes and tears fell down his cheeks.

"I had to come to see you, Danny. I know you are there. I know where you would hide. You stood on this boulder and said your morning prayer, didn't you?"

Danny stepped from behind the boulder. There stood his father.

"Son, I had to see that you were safe," his father said.

"I came here for the same reason," Danny said. "I had to make sure you were safe. And mother, and Jeanne, too." His father reached for him and pulled Danny to his chest. "It is so good to see you, son. Your grandfather sang songs for you. Rick gave us news of you. He told us you had a plan to escape."

"Did he tell you about the coffin?" Danny asked.

"Yes," his father said. "Your grandfather did not like that plan. But he is ready for your healing ceremony."

"I will be so glad to be free of the death," Danny said. "Did Rick tell you about the slave traders?"

"Some, but he said you had many stories to tell." Then Danny asked the question he was most afraid to ask. "Is Jeanne well?"

"Yes, Danny. She is weak from the fever," he said, "but she is well. We don't drink the water they bring for us. It's making people sick. Some are dying. We boil the water and sift it through cloth. It is better."

"Jim Davis told me it's safe now back home, at Canyon de Chelly. He said Navajo people are hiding in the caves. Father, we need to go home."

"Yes, son, I know."

"Can you escape at night?"

"Danny, escaping from the fort would not be hard to do. People are sleeping outside the fort, with few guards to watch over them."

"Then why do they stay?"

"The real danger is not the water or the soldiers. The real danger is not starving to death. The bands of outlaws are the real danger. They look for healthy people to capture and sell as slaves. You met them, Danny. Would you want your mother and sister to face the slave traders in the desert, with no horses or weapons?"

"No," Danny said. "You are better staying here. But what can we do?"

"I don't know, Danny. Stay alive for now. Maybe your friends can help us."

"They are good friends," said Danny. "They are smart and strong. Yes, we will come up with a plan."

"Rick says for you to stay here for a few days," his father said. "Don't try to find us. We will come to you. He also said to move about. Sleep somewhere else tonight, but nearby, so we can find you."

"I will be careful," Danny said. "Will you come tomorrow?"

"Yes, and maybe I'll bring your grandfather tomorrow. He wants to see you, Danny."

"I want to see him, too. Will you tell him I only climbed in the coffin so I could see you, all of you, again?"

"Yes, Danny. He understands. Now I'm going back to the fort. Look for us before sunrise tomorrow."

Danny watched as his father climbed to the top of the small hill and disappeared. He wrapped his arms around himself and closed his eyes. For the first time in many months, Danny was truly happy.

"Now," he said to himself, "I need to be more careful than ever. The soldiers from Fort Davis are looking for me. Manny is looking for me. And rattlesnakes just won't leave me alone!"

He touched his calf and remembered being bitten by a rattlesnake only a few months ago. A bullying prisoner had put the snake in Danny's bed. When Danny had climbed under the covers to go to sleep, the rattlesnake sank his fangs into Danny's leg.

Danny spent the day exploring the hills and canyon surrounding the fort. Just before sunset he climbed a steep hill and crouched low behind a clump of bushes. When he stood up, a huge lake lay before him. Danny wiped his dry lips. *Water! Finally*!

But something was different about this lake. No waves lapped the shore. No one fished at the edge of the lake. No boats floated on it. No fish jumped from the water, and no birds dipped from the sky.

The lake did not sparkle in the light of the setting sun. The water was a dirty white color. On the far side, not far from the fort, Danny saw soldiers filling leather bags with water from the lake.

"That is the poison water that made my sister sick," he whispered. "The water in those bags will make other Navajo people sick. I cannot let that happen, not today."

Danny watched as the soldiers tossed the filled water bags on a flatbed wagon. Most of the bags were empty.

"They are just beginning," he said. "I have time."

He ran down the hill, dodging cactus plants and sharp rocks. When he reached the bottom, he sprinted around the lake. After a short while, he stopped to catch his breath. He slowly climbed the hill. He was close to the soldiers now.

Now is the time to be very careful and quiet, he thought. *They might have a guard watching over the workers.*

Danny was right. A guard was nearby, resting in the shade of a scrubby tree. His back was to the wagon. Danny spotted the guard and jumped behind a boulder.

He's not expecting any trouble, Danny thought. The guard pulled the brim of his hat over his head.

"He is going to sleep," he whispered to himself. "Now is my time. I'll cut the bags so they can't carry the poison water."

Danny crept from the hill, one careful step at a time. He knelt down and listened. He walked behind the wagon, away from the guard, with the wagon between himself and the lake.

He lifted his knife from its hiding place on his right calf. He crawled to the edge of the wagon and slowly pulled himself over the side.

"How many more bags we got to fill?" a voice called out.

"Too many," a soldier replied. "Maybe twenty, maybe more."

"Bring 'em to me," the first soldier said.

Danny froze. The empty bags were piled all around him, on the bed of the wagon where he hid.

Chapter 11
Grandfather to the Rescue

Danny's eyes darted from one side of the wagon to the other. There was no place to hide and no time anyway. The soldier neared the wagon. He was ten steps from discovering Danny.

What if they recognize me? Danny wondered. *What if they send me back to Fort Davis?* Danny shook with fear at the thought of returning to Fort Davis. *They think I stole the horse. They hang horse thieves!*

"We don't need to fill every bag," the soldier said, looking over his shoulder.

"Fine, just bring me an armload," came the reply. "It's getting too hot for a man to live out here. We'll fill a few more and leave."

Danny closed his eyes and waited. He expected a shout at least, maybe even gunfire. Any minute he knew he would be seen.

I will be tied at the wrists and ankles and brought before an officer.

Danny Blackgoat was wrong. Instead, he heard another set of footsteps.

"Do you men need some help?" A voice floated from the morning and hovered over him. Danny smiled and nodded his head.

"Yes, yes, Grandfather," he whispered. "You are always there when I need you. Always."

"You can't help us, old man," the soldier said, turning away from the wagon. "What are you doing this far from the fort? It's not safe for you out here!"

"I'm not too old to work," Danny's grandfather said. "Here, I'll bring the bags to you."

Danny's grandfather stepped in front of the soldier and grabbed an armful of bags.

"Here," he said. "Go ahead, now. I'll bring the rest."

The soldiers laughed. "You are one lucky old Indian man," said one. "Most soldiers would just leave you out here for the buzzards."

"I'm not afraid of buzzards," said Grandfather. "I'm an old man. I'm like a buzzard."

The soldiers laughed again.

He is making friends with them, Danny thought. *Maybe that's the smart thing to do, at least for now.*

As he lay without moving on the wagon bed, Danny remembered his old friend, Jim Davis. *He is so much like my grandfather,* he thought. *Both of them make friends instead of enemies.*

As he leaned over for the the bags, Grandfather nodded to him.

"Shhhh," he whispered. Danny wanted to leap from the wagon and hold his grandfather close to his chest. He was so happy to see him. Instead, he met his eyes, then lowered his gaze out of respect.

"When I holler, you run," Grandfather whispered.

Danny nodded without speaking. His grandfather carried the bags to the lakeshore.

"Bags," he said to the soldiers, stacking the bags and pointing. "Bags for water."

He is acting like a clown, thought Danny. *The soldiers are laughing.*

As he turned to the wagon for more bags, his grandfather fell to the ground.

"Yowwww!" he shouted. He rolled down the slope to the water. "No swim," he called out. "Help!"

The soldiers never stopped laughing.

"What do you think?" said one. "Should we help him or just watch him sink?"

"The water's bad enough without bodies floating around in it," said the other. "Drag the old man to the wagon. Let's get back to the fort."

By the time the soldiers lifted his grandfather and carried him to the wagon, Danny was gone. He dashed to the top of the hill and watched as the soldiers tossed the water bags—and his grandfather—to the wagon bed.

"The safe thing to do would be to hide until dark," Danny said to himself. "But I have never done the safe thing. I'm following my grandfather."

From the hilltop, Danny hid in the shadows of thorny trees. He trailed after the wagon, watching it bump and bounce. His grandfather rolled from side to side.

"Poor Grandfather," he whispered.

Soon the soldiers came to a stop, outside the gates of the fort. Fort Sumner was surrounded by small campsites. Hundreds of Navajo people huddled against the walls of the fort. They leaned against trees. But the trees had no branches or leaves. Most of the trees were even stripped of bark. *They are using anything they can find for firewood*, thought Danny.

Grandfather crawled over the side of the wagon. He waved to the soldiers and they laughed and shouted, "Remember, old man. You're a buzzard, not a fish! We might not pull you out of the water next time!"

As soon as they were gone, Grandfather pointed to a group of Navajos against a nearby tree. *He is telling me where my family is*, Danny thought. A warm smile crept across his face. *Now is the time to be safe. I can see my family after dark.*

Danny crept down the hill. He made his way to his hiding place near the rattlesnake cave. By the mouth of the cave he spotted a leather bag. A trail of ants climbed in and out of the bag.

"Rick left me a water bag," Danny said. "He's the only one who knows where I am. I hope he didn't reach inside the cave." Danny walked as quietly as he could to the cave, grabbed the bag, and ran to his sleeping spot.

"No, Rick is too smart to reach inside a cave," he said to himself. "He knows something would claim it as a home."

He brushed the ants from the bag and untied the leather string at the opening. *My first drink since I left the Gradys'*, he thought.

He balanced the bag on his right palm and circled his left fingers around the leather mouth hole. Slowly lifting the bag, he took several long gulps, swallowing every drop before he lowered the bag.

"Ummmm," he said, wiping his lips with his tongue. That's when he noticed a funny taste to the water.

It tastes like soup, he thought. *Beef soup.* He stretched the bag open and saw five thick strips of dried beef.

Rick, what a surprise! You're feeding my thirst and my hunger both. Oh, now I understand. That's why the ants were crawling in the bag. They smelled the beef. I don't blame them. I'd swim in a lake, too, for Rick's dried beef.

With his belly full of beef and good, clean water from Fort Davis, Danny leaned against the tree.

I have had a good day, he thought. *I saw my grandfather. Rick is watching out for me. But none of this would have happened without my good friend Jim Davis. I hope he is well.*

He decided to take an afternoon nap. As he fell asleep, he whispered a prayer for his friend.

Danny hoped to wake up before sunset, but he didn't realize how tired he was. He slept soundly until well after dark. He awoke to the sound of a voice only a few feet behind him. The clouds covered the moon and Danny lay unseen, on the other side of the tree.

"Are you sure there ain't no soldiers keeping watch?" a man asked.

"*No, hablo la verdad,*" said another man. "I speak the truth."

Danny dropped his jaw. His body jerked, and he felt the cold breath of fear.

The second voice belonged to Manny.

Chapter 12
Danny's Promise

Manny has new gang members, Danny thought. *I wonder how many.*

In a moment he had his answer. The clouds parted and he saw four men on horseback. They stood high in their saddles and looked down at the fort.

"Now is the best time to raid the camp," Manny said. "The Navajos have no weapons. They are too hungry and too sick to fight, even if they had weapons."

Danny felt angry to hear his people being thought of so lightly. But he knew what Manny said was true. His people could not protect themselves.

"No!" he said aloud, then slapped his hand over his mouth. He hoped no one had heard him.

They thought I was helpless at Fort Davis. Danny's mind was racing. *But my friend came up with a plan. Maybe we can't fight them with weapons. But we are smart. We can still win.*

He lay still and waited. When Manny and his men rode away, Danny followed, running in the shadows. *They've never been here*, he thought. *They'll ride slowly, and I can keep up with them.*

Soon Manny and his men topped the hill overlooking the lake. Danny crept closer and crouched behind a boulder to listen.

"*Mira, como dije*," Manny said, pointing at the camps below. "No guards, like I told you. We can ride into the camp. They won't expect us. Each of us can capture an Indian. The ones that fight the most, those are the ones we want. They are young and will bring the most money."

Manny was pointing to the camps near Danny's family.

"Let's water the horses first," Manny said. "After we catch the Indians, we might have a long ride. They don't have horses, but they'll chase us on foot."

I have to warn them, Danny thought.

While Manny and his men rode to the lake, Danny dashed down the hill. He saw his family sitting in the shade of blankets stretched over a tree. He ducked under the blankets.

"Grandfather!" he shouted. "They are coming."

His father stood. "Who is coming?" he asked. "The soldiers?"

"No, far worse," Danny said, shaking his head. "The men who took me. They capture people and sell them to be slaves. They are watering their horses now. But it won't be long. They have guns. They will be here!"

"We should let everyone know," his grandfather said.

"Will the soldiers help us?" Danny asked.

"Maybe," Grandfather said. "But we cannot be sure."

"Mother, I am free," Danny whispered.

"Yes, son," she said, pulling him close for a brief moment. "Now, take us to a safe place."

Danny helped his sister Jeanne to her feet. "Stay with me, Jeanne. We'll be all right."

Then Danny turned to his grandfather. "Do you know of a place where we can hide?" he asked.

"Yes." He pointed to a high hill, on the other side of an arroyo. "Every morning I go there to pray. It's a steep climb," he said, "but if I can do it, we all can."

"Danny, take the family to the praying spot. I'm going to let the others know," his father said. Danny nodded.

More Navajos than he had ever seen surrounded the fort—more than when Danny and his family arrived at the fort almost a year ago. Danny's father moved from one camp to another, shouting a warning.

Danny took Jeanne by the hand. "Let's go," he said. "Walk fast but watch every step. Remember, snakes are out at night."

As Danny and his family hurried to the arroyo, his father yelled loud enough for a thousand Navajos to hear. "The raiders are coming!" he shouted. "They are here! Hide your children. The slave traders are here!"

Danny looked over his shoulder. In the dim light of the moon he saw people rising and moving about. *They have no place to go*, he thought.

"Danny," Grandfather said, "watch where you are going. We are following you now. Remember that. You are our leader."

His grandfather had never called him a leader before. No one had ever called Danny Blackgoat a leader. But in one year, Danny had grown from a tough young man who fought with his fists to a strong young leader who fought with his thinking.

Danny walked quickly to the edge of the arroyo. He paused and looked down at the steep canyon walls.

"Grandfather?" he asked.

"That way," Grandfather said, pointing to a narrow path beside a clump of sage bushes. Danny nodded and gripped his sister's hand.

"Don't be afraid," he said. "We will be safe soon."

Jeanne squeezed his hand hard. With his mother and grandfather behind him, Danny began the dangerous climb down the arroyo wall. Danny's foot hit a loose rock and he slipped and fell backwards.

"Careful," he said over his shoulder.

He tried to grab a bush, but yanked it from the dirt. He rolled down the path to the bottom of the canyon. Dusting himself off, he stood and helped the others. Soon they all stood on the canyon floor.

Danny was searching the opposite wall for a place to climb when the first gunshots exploded.

Pow! Pow! Pow! Pow!

He heard screams coming from the Navajo camps. He looked to his grandfather.

"We can only help them if we are still alive," his grandfather said. He pointed to the path before them.

"But where is my father?" Danny asked. He stared at the canyon wall behind him, hoping to see his father hurrying down the path. He saw no one.

Pow! Pow!

Gunshots echoed through the canyon. Danny's mother stopped. She looked at Danny, bowed her head and spoke.

"Danny, when we saw you tied to the horse like a saddle, I wanted to run to you. I had to hold your father back."

"The soldiers would have shot you both," said Danny.

"Yes," she nodded, "and they will shoot you now if you try to help. Your father knows where we are going. He will find us. You have to believe that."

"One day I will have a horse of my own," Danny said. He took a deep breath and looked to the path in front of him. "I will have a weapon to protect my family. I will have friends that ride with me. I will not wait for soldiers to come, or raiders to come."

"Danny," his grandfather said, "I believe you. I believe you are strong and will use what you have learned to help us. But you must stay alive."

"My father needs me," said Danny.

"Your father needs you here, with us. If you run to the gunshots, you make your father's job harder."

"You are right, Grandfather," Danny said. But he never forgot the promise he made to himself: *I will not always run away.*

Chapter 13
Grandfather's Healing

Leaving the Navajo camps behind them, Danny and his family climbed the path and found a site high on the mesa overlooking the fort. Juniper trees poked up from a boulder, casting long shadows across the ground.

"This is a safe place for now," Grandfather said. Jeanne and Danny's mother broke leafy branches from the trees and swept the ground.

"Sweep good, Jeanne," their mother said. "We don't want to sit on scorpions or spiders."

Soon Danny's family was settled, leaning against the boulder.

"Mother, Grandfather," Danny said, "please trust me. I will not go to the camp. I won't try to rescue anybody. Not today. But we cannot stay here for long without water."

"The lake is a long way from here," said his mother.

"And you know the water is not good to drink," His grandfather said. "It's what made your sister sick."

"Rick brought me good water yesterday," Danny said. "He will get us water from the fort, the water the soldiers drink. Let me find him."

Danny's mother closed her eyes. "We are safe, Danny. Sit down and be with us. The water can wait." Danny was not one to argue with his mother. He sat beside her. She put her hand to his cheek.

"I have missed you, Danny," she said. "I prayed for you every day. I was so afraid for you."

"Grandfather," Danny said. "I am afraid we will never be safe. I have something to tell you."

"You have been close to death," Grandfather said. "I knew it when I saw you climb into the wagon at the lake."

"What can you do?" Danny asked. He had learned, long ago, that death was evil and must be avoided. When a Navajo dies inside their hogan, their home, the body is quickly buried and everyone moves away. "Can you help me?"

"Yes," Grandfather said. "We must cleanse you of death. Tonight we will have a healing ceremony."

The Blackgoat family huddled together, high above the screams and gunshots from the camp below. Every throat burned, but no one mentioned water again. When the sun dipped behind the mountains, Grandfather knelt down and scratched out a circle in the sand with a stone. He took Danny by the palms and led him to the center of the circle.

"Sit down, Danny," he said. "Everyone gather around the circle."

Danny never saw his grandfather take the rattle from his pocket. He closed his eyes and listened to the sweet shaking sound of the rattle, soon joined by Grandfather's voice.

The old man turned slowly, moving around the circle, singing his healing chant.

Danny slumped over and rested his chin on his chest. To anyone watching, he looked to be asleep. He was dreaming, dreams he would never share with anyone.

The night was long and dark. Grandfather sang and circled behind the family. The shifting sound of his rattle whispered a soft rhythm. He moved more slowly as the hours passed, and his voice fell to a whisper.

As morning neared and streaks of red lined the horizon, Danny opened his eyes. His hand went to the leather pouch around his neck. He looked to Grandfather.

"You may bless the morning," Grandfather said. He took Danny's arms and lifted him to his feet.

Danny felt every muscle of his body as if for the first time. He flexed his fingers. He stretched his arms high over his head. He moved his ankles back and forth to make sure his feet still worked.

He took a deep breath before taking his first step, like a child learning to walk. After a few steps he turned to face his family. Everyone looked to him. His mother smiled.

Danny walked quietly away from his family. Facing the morning sun, he said his prayer.

When morning casts its light on the canyon wall

A new house is made,

A house made of dawn.

Before me, everything is beautiful

Behind me, everything is beautiful

Above me, everything is beautiful

Below me, everything is beautiful

Around me, everything is beautiful

Within me, everything is beautiful.

Taja ahotahe, nothing will change.

As he glanced down at the fort, Danny saw flames rising from the camp. He remembered the first morning the soldiers came. They burned the Navajo homes, the hogans. They destroyed the cornfields. They killed his sheep.

"Now Manny and his men have come to hurt us. I will be strong enough someday to stop them," he said aloud.

"Yes, son. Someday," a voice behind him said. Danny turned to face his father. "I am proud of you, son," his father said, pulling him close to his chest. Danny felt a warm breeze blow over them.

"I was afraid for you," he said. "We all were. I wanted to look for you. Mother wouldn't let me go."

"Your mother is smart, Danny. One of the raiders was asking for you. He said your name over and over. What did you do to make him so angry?"

"His name is Manny," said Danny. "His men were going to kill Rick. They knocked him out and were about to kill him. I told Manny to let Rick live. I told him I would take him to a place with young people. People they could take as slaves."

"Did you do that?"

"No, Father. I lied to Manny. I led them to a ranch with guards and rifles. All of his men were killed. Only Manny escaped."

"Danny," his father said, "you have seen too much death."

"Yes. And I have done things I never thought I would do."

"You know that Manny will never stop looking for you, don't you?"

Danny waited for a long moment before speaking. He looked to the ground. When he lifted his eyes, he had left Manny behind him. His thoughts moved to his family.

"Father, we need water," he said. "Rick left water and food for me at my hiding place. He will do it every day, I know he will. I have to return."

"Danny, I don't want to lose you again. But Manny and his men are gone."

"Did they take anyone?"

"Yes, son. They left with three young Navajos. Two girls and a boy your age."

"No one will notice me if I go now," Danny said. "They have their own families. Please let me go. I will be careful."

"You are alive, Danny. So I know you have learned their ways. Yes, go now. I will tell your mother."

Chapter 14
In the Shadow of Death

Danny gave one last look over his shoulder. His family was huddled together, hiding in the shadows from the scorching sun. Danny slid down the path and hurried up the canyon wall.

Soon he walked among the Navajo camps. Children cried and men and women helped their neighbors put their fires out. Danny passed unnoticed through the hundreds of campsites. When he reached the hilltop overlooking the lake, he crouched down.

Now I must be careful, he thought.

He scanned the lake from shore to shore. He saw no one. Finally, he rose and hurried to the far side of the lake. He cast his gaze over the lake and camps and surrounding hills.

Convinced he was alone, Danny ran to the mouth of the rattlesnake cave, his hiding place. As he hoped, Rick had returned and left two large leather bags.

"Enough water and food for my family," Danny said aloud.

"That's what I was hoping for," said Rick. Danny jumped to hear his voice. Rick was sitting in the cave.

"Rattlesnakes live there!" Danny shouted. "You better be careful."

"Not anymore they don't," said Rick. "I smoked them out last night. They didn't mind leaving. But they made me promise to scare you before they left."

"That's not funny," Danny said. "I am tired of people sneaking up on me."

"You make it so easy," Rick said, laughing. "You always look over your shoulder. Maybe somebody is smart enough to know where you're going, and they beat you there."

Danny smiled. "I won't forgive you for scaring me. Not yet. But I do thank you for the food and water."

"You're welcome," said Rick. "I brought enough for your family. But we need to talk about something else, Danny."

"What?"

"You remember the talk about Jim Davis being in danger?"

"For stealing Fire Eye?" Danny asked.

"Yes," Rick said. "Stealing a horse is a very serious crime. Davis is already a prisoner, so he won't get a trial. Besides, this is wartime. If they think he stole Fire Eye, he will hang."

"He stole him for me," Danny said, "so I could escape from the graveyard. I'm the one who rode away on Fire Eye!" Danny said.

"But Jim Davis stole him, Danny. You've got to remember, this is a war between the Army of the North and the rebel states of the South. Jim Davis is a prisoner of war. Some of the officers at the fort would like any excuse to hang a rebel. Now they have one."

"Jim Davis was my best friend at Fort Davis," Danny said. "He taught me to speak your language. He planned my escape. What can I do to help him?"

"Danny, you can't do anything. If they decide Jim Davis is innocent, who will they think is guilty?"

Danny realized for the first time that his life was in danger.

"Me," he said quietly. "If they catch me, they could hang me."

"Yes," Rick said. "The only thing you can do is stay hidden—from Manny and from the soldiers. Stay out of sight."

"I was going to bring water to my family. They are on the mesa, above the camps."

"I'll make sure they have food and water. You need to stay away for a few days, until things settle down. The soldiers will be prowling all over these hills, looking for Manny and his men. I cleaned this cave out for you, Danny. So you'd have a place to sleep."

"Thank you," Danny said. "Will you let my family know I am safe?"

"I will," Rick promised. "I'll take food and water to them now."

Soon Danny was alone, sitting on the floor of the cave. He leaned against the wall and fell asleep. He spent the next few days discovering new hiding places. *It's only safe if I don't stay here all the time,* he thought.

He found a safe lookout over the road. He watched the wagons roll in and out of Fort Sumner. On the morning of the third day, Danny spotted Rick's wagon leaving the gates of the fort. As Rick drew closer, Danny stared at Rick's two horses pulling the wagon. Something was different.

"Fire Eye!" he whispered. As he watched, Fire Eye danced from side to side.

"He looks like he wants to run," Danny said. "Maybe he will. Today."

He glanced up and down the road. Seeing no one, he waited for Rick to pass below a rock overhang. When he did, Danny leaped from the rock to the seat beside Rick.

"Whoa!" Rick shouted. He jerked the reins in surprise and turned to Danny.

"All right, son," he said. "I guess that makes us even. Just don't try that again. I was about to jump off the wagon and let you have it."

"That's what I was hoping," Danny laughed. Rick patted him on the back.

"Good to have you along, Danny Blackgoat," he said. "Any special reason you joined me?"

"I saw Fire Eye and I had to jump," Danny said. "Can I ride him tonight?"

"Sounds good to me."

"Maybe we can see the Gradys," Danny said. "They saved both of us from Manny and his men."

"That's a good idea, Danny. I'd like to meet them."

Just before nightfall, they approached the Grady ranch.

"It's not far now," Danny said, pointing to the path leading to the watering hole.

As the dark settled over the desert, Rick pulled his wagon to the roadside.

"Now I can ride Fire Eye," Danny said. "He'll be glad to see Sarah."

Danny stepped from the wagon and took Fire Eye by the reins.

"Maybe tonight's not a good night, Danny," Rick said. His voice was serious.

"Why not?"

"Look," Rick replied. He was pointing to the sky over the Grady ranch. Long columns of dark smoke curled over the hill. "There's been a fire, Danny. Looks like a bad one."

"No!" Danny called out. "Not the Gradys!"

"Manny is not the kind of man to forget," Rick said. "The Gradys killed his men."

"If I thought he would go after the Gradys, I would have shot him when I had the chance," Danny said. He gritted his teeth and clenched his fists. "This is my fault," he said, fighting back tears as he spoke. "All of it. Jim Davis's trouble. And now the Gradys." Danny untied Fire Eye from the wagon.

"I have to go, Rick. Don't try to stop me. I have to see if they are still alive."

"I'm going with you. Let's hide the wagon as best we can."

They found a dark spot behind a boulder and parked the wagon. Rick saddled his horse and said to Danny, "Sorry I don't have a saddle for you. I wasn't expecting you."

Danny wrapped his arms around Fire Eye's neck and leaped onto his back. Fire Eye stomped the ground and whinnied.

"I think he's glad to see you," said Rick.

"Easy, boy," Danny said. He patted Fire Eye's neck. "We'll go slow and easy."

"Wait," Rick said. He reached under the wagon seat and pulled out two shotguns. "They are both loaded," he said, handing one to Danny.

Rick followed Danny up the steep hill. They steered the horses carefully, stepping over rocks and cactus plants. As they topped the hill, they pulled the horses to a halt. A half-moon lit the scene below.

Fresh water gurgled and splashed. The yellow moonlight on the water was a beautiful sight to see. But beyond the woods, in the direction of the ranch house, the sky was bright with fire.

"It's not safe to ride to the spring," Danny said in a quiet voice. "They might be hiding in the woods. We should circle the spring and stay out of sight."

Rick nodded. They eased their horses down the hill. They avoided the woods and rode around the spring. As they neared the house, Danny urged Fire Eye into a gallop. Spirals of smoke rose from the ranch house and the barn.

"Nooo," he muttered. "Please, no."

The ranch house was burned to the ground. Danny jumped from Fire Eye and ran to the back of the house. Two long logs, burning from top to bottom, shaped an *X* across what had been the back door.

The stone fireplace stood straight and tall. Flaming boards cracked and crashed around it. The smell of smoke was everywhere. Danny coughed and waved the smoke from his face. He took a step and stumbled on the outside dining table. He fell to his knees and rolled across the burning table.

Rick lifted Danny to his feet.

"Careful where you step, Danny," he said.

Danny remembered his meal with the Gradys. *The Gradys saved my life,* he thought. *I hope they are safe.*

They heard a loud crashing sound behind them. They turned and saw the roof of the barn collapse.

"I wonder where everyone is." Rick said.

They climbed on their horses and circled the burning barn. They saw no one.

Finally, Danny pointed to the woods. "Maybe that way," he shouted, and they rode in the direction of the spring.

As Danny entered the woods, he gripped Fire Eye's mane and pulled him to a slow walk. In the dim light of the moon, he saw Mr. Grady lying face down on the ground.

Danny slid from his horse and walked slowly to Mr. Grady, hoping with every step that Grady would roll over. Danny picked up a broken branch and touched his boot heel. Grady did not move.

"He's gone, Danny," said Rick. "There's nothing you can do about it."

Danny stepped away from Mr. Grady. He remembered his grandfather's words before the healing ceremony: *You have been too close to death.*

Chapter 15
Blood and Water

Danny turned his back to Grady and walked away, in the direction of the spring. He did not stop to see if Manny or his men were watering their horses.

"Danny," Rick whispered, following after him. "Be careful. Manny could be anywhere."

Danny ignored his friend. He walked faster and faster, as if he could outrun his feelings and the image of Mr. Grady lying on the ground.

Danny stepped from the woods and walked to the sparkling spring. The moon shone bright and anyone could see him.

But Danny was not thinking about safety. He was thinking about revenge.

"They have hurt and killed too many good people, Rick," he said. "Manny needs to pay for what he has done."

"Stop for a minute, Danny, and think," Rick said. He was breathing hard from trying to keep up with his younger friend. "What does Manny hope you'll do?"

"He hopes I'll forget about this. He hopes I'll go away and forget."

Rick sat down on a rock and dipped his hands in the water. He took a drink and spoke in a quiet voice.

"Think about it, Danny," he said. "What would Manny really want?"

Danny shook his head back and forth. Tears flowed down his cheeks. He wiped them away and sat beside Rick.

"Manny wants me to come after him, doesn't he?" he said.

"Yes, son. Manny would like nothing better than to capture you. I don't want to think about what he would do. To both of us. He had a chance to kill us both. Instead, he believed you, and it got his men killed."

"I am paying for my lies," Danny whispered.

"I don't know about that, Danny. But we need to have a plan before we start chasing Manny. Can we agree on that?"

"Yes," said Danny. "Thank you for being my friend."

"Now," Rick said as he stood, "let's get back to our horses."

"Just a minute," Danny said. "Sarah always kept a cup for drinking by the spring. I want to try one last time to help Mr. Grady."

He found the tin cup nailed to a nearby tree and filled it with spring water. Rick walked behind as Danny returned to Mr. Grady.

He's dead, Rick thought, *but Danny needs a last good-bye.*

Danny walked slowly to Mr. Grady. He knelt beside him. He closed his eyes and lifted his head to the night sky.

Danny remembered the day, long ago, when he had saved Jim Davis's life. Davis had felt a burning pain in his chest. The other prisoners were going to let him die. But

Danny had brought him back to life. He had pounded on Davis's chest and had blown air into his mouth to help him breathe. He had never given up on his friend. *And I will not give up on Mr. Grady*, Danny thought.

He opened his eyes. Rick stood beside him. His hands were folded across his belly and his head was bowed.

"Rick!" Danny said. Rick looked up in surprise.

"What? What's happening?" He turned to his horse and pulled his shotgun from the saddle.

"No," Danny said. "Nobody is here. It's just the three of us. You, me, and Mr. Grady."

"What do you mean?"

"Mr. Grady is alive." Danny rolled Mr. Grady on his back. He tilted the cup to his lips and pulled his jaw open. He poured a thin stream of water into Grady's mouth. For a few seconds, nothing happened. The water just dribbled from his mouth.

"Help me lift him," Danny said. Rick held Grady from behind and raised him from the ground. Danny poured another stream of water into his mouth. Grady spit it out, all over Danny!

"Yes!" Danny shouted. Mr. Grady coughed and sputtered. Without thinking, Danny tossed the cup at him, splashing his face and chest with cold spring water.

Grady blinked his eyes. He rocked back and forth, and finally sat up straight.

Rick dropped his jaw. He looked from Danny to Grady and back again.

"What happened?" Grady asked. "Where is my family?" He closed his eyes again and touched his temple. Danny gasped. Grady had a knot as big as a peach on the side of his head. It was dark purple and covered with dried blood.

"Danny, he needs help," Rick said. He ripped Grady's shirt from his back. Red blood flowed from an open wound in his shoulder. "Let's get him to the spring."

Rick and Danny carried Mr. Grady to a leafy patch of ground in the trees by the spring. For several hours they tended to his gunshot wound.

"First, we need to get that shell out of him," Rick said.

Danny held him still while Rick dug the shell from his shoulder.

"Bring me a handful of mud and dried leaves," Rick said.

He patted the mixture on the bleeding bullet hole. When the blood finally stopped flowing, Rick leaned against a tree trunk.

"Now," he said softly, "we wait."

Rick soon fell asleep against the tree, and only his loud snoring kept Danny awake. At the first sign of morning, Danny walked to the spring. He looked to the sky and reached for his pouch of corn pollen.

As the sun rose yellow and strong, he whispered the morning prayer.

Chapter 16
Mr. Grady's Story

"He's going to make it, Danny," Rick said, as Danny returned.

"How can you tell?"

"The blood is all dried. There's nothing fresh," Rick said. "So it's stopped flowing. Now, Danny, get close to him and tell me what you hear. Go on, get close to his face."

Danny knelt beside Grady and leaned close. He saw Grady's lips open and close, but so slightly that no one would ever notice. Then he saw his chest move up and down.

"He is breathing. He is alive," Danny said. "I will never forget what you have done."

"My family will remember, too," said Mr. Grady. His eyes were open and he nodded to Danny.

"Mr. Grady," Danny said, "we were so afraid for you and your family."

"Did you see any sign of them?" Grady asked.

"There were no bodies," said Rick. "They are still alive, that's what we think. Manny probably took them."

"This is my friend Rick," Danny said. "He saved you." Rick stood and shook Grady's hand.

"We will do everything we can to help you," Rick said. "Manny tried to kill us too. But Danny says you folks saved him."

"Yes." Grady said, "That was quite a battle. We won that one, but men like Manny never forget."

"That's what I've been telling Danny. Maybe the three of us will have a chance."

"Did you see Sarah before they shot you?" Danny asked.

"Yes, I saw her running this way. I rode my horse after her. Manny shot me. The last thing I saw before I hit the ground was Sarah. Manny caught her. He grabbed her by the waist and rode across the spring."

"Mr. Grady," Danny said, "we have enemies everywhere. But we also have good friends, people like Rick. Sarah is alive. I know it. And we will find her."

"Thank you, Danny Blackgoat," Grady said. "I believe you."

"Can you tell us what happened?" Rick asked.

Mr. Grady took a long, deep breath. He ran his hand through his hair and hung his head on his chest. When he spoke his voice was quiet. He was reliving the memory as he told the story.

"Just before sunrise yesterday, one of my ranch hands woke me up. He was guarding the spring that night. He said some men were stealing cattle. I told him to get a group together and follow them. Manny was behind it, I know that now. He wanted my men gone so he could take my family.

"As soon as the men rode over the hill after the cattle thieves, I heard gunfire. I don't know how many were captured, or how many were killed. But when none of my men returned, I knew this was bad, very bad. My wife and Sarah hid in the house. I took my gun and climbed to a loft in the barn.

"Manny must have circled the woods. He attacked from the front of the house. I couldn't see him. I heard screaming and ran to the house. It was already burning. Next thing I knew, Sarah was running from the burning house, heading to the spring. I followed her, like I said. That's when Manny shot me."

When he finished his story, Mr. Grady looked up at us, like he was seeing us for the first time. He shook his head back and forth.

"I should have made sure my family was safe," he said.

"Grady," Rick said, "I have a family, too. A wife and a daughter Danny's age. They're at Fort Davis right now. But I sometimes take them on the road above your ranch. I always thought it was safe. With Manny out there, and others like him, nothing is safe. You can't blame yourself for this. We will bring your family back."

"Why would you help me?" Grady asked.

"Because you saved my life," Danny said. "And something else. Mr. Grady, Manny would never have burned your house if I hadn't brought him here."

"I guess we're all gonna feel guilty," Grady said. "You're right, Rick. Let's find my family."

Grady reached his hands out and Rick helped him to his feet.

"I think we should wait a few days, Grady, till you're able to ride. You almost died, you know."

"We don't have time to wait," said Grady. "I can get well while we ride."

"We've only got two horses," Rick said.

"Manny doesn't know everything about the Grady ranch. I know where I can find a good, fast horse. He's too jumpy to help out on the ranch, but I can ride him. Whenever there's noise, he hides in the boulders across the way." Grady pointed to a spot on the far side of the ranch.

In less than an hour, Grady had caught and saddled his horse, Solo. They filled their bags with water and climbed the hills in search of Manny, Mrs. Grady, and Sarah. They rode without speaking until they reached the woods overlooking the ranch.

"I was afraid of that," Grady said. He stepped from Solo and walked in the direction of two bodies in a clump of juniper trees. "Two of my best men."

Danny had seen enough death to know what had to be done.

"I'll find a shovel," he said to Rick. He rode back to the barn while Rick and Grady tended to the bodies. Grady could not keep himself from weeping.

"We had a good life here," he said. "It was hard work, but we had warm beds in the winter and plenty of food. Now that's all gone. At least for these two."

He washed the faces of the men. He laid them side by side, brushing the dust from their clothes. He took his hat off and prayed over them. Soon Danny returned with a shovel. Taking turns, Rick and Danny dug two shallow graves.

Danny stepped to the shadows as the men lifted the bodies and settled them into their final resting place. He watched as Mr. Grady sang a burial song.

Following the burial of two of his best men, Grady rode with a new urgency. No one had to say it. They all knew that unless they found Sarah and her mother soon, they might have to bury them as well.

Chapter 17
Manny's Camp

Manny left an easy trail to follow. The horse tracks led across the road and into the barren desert country.

Less than a mile from the road, the tracks went three different directions.

"What's going on?" Grady asked.

"They've split up," said Rick, "so they can't be followed."

"How can we know which one is Manny? He's got Sarah," said Grady.

Several tracks led west of the road, toward Fort Sumner. Tracks of several more horses led east. Only one set of tracks continued south, to the desert.

The men stepped from their horses.

"You know Manny would take the most men with him," said Grady. "I'd say we follow these tracks, going west."

Danny was on his knees studying the tracks. "Mr. Grady," he said, "Manny is a tall, heavy man. And he was carrying Sarah. Look at the tracks of the single horse."

Rick and Grady knelt beside him.

"These tracks are deeper than the others. The rider was heavier. And Manny is smart. He knows we would think he would never go alone. This is Manny's horse," Danny said. He stood slowly and waited.

"You always surprise me, Danny," Rick said. His voice had a quiet tone of respect. "How did you know to study tracks so close to the ground?"

"No one taught me," Danny said. "I guess it was from taking care of my sheep. I could tell which sheep was missing by the tracks."

"Well, you've outsmarted Manny again," Rick said. "Let's go!"

"Just a minute," Grady said. "I agree with Danny. Manny is riding into the desert. He probably has a camp there."

"Then let's go," Rick said.

Mr. Grady said nothing. He turned his head slowly to Rick and lowered his eyes.

I have never seen him look so sad, Danny thought.

"You are thinking of Mrs. Grady," Rick finally said. "You do not want to choose." Grady nodded.

"I will not choose," he whispered.

"Grady," Rick said, "we know Manny has Sarah. Manny is taking the quickest way to the camp. But by night, the other men will be there, too. Your wife and Sarah both will be there. Let's be there before the others."

Grady nodded and mounted Solo. With Danny and Rick following, he urged his horse into a gallop. Manny was so sure he would not be followed, he did nothing to hide his tracks. With the soft snowfall of the night before, his horse left deep tracks in the snow.

"Looks like he stopped to rest here," Grady said. He pointed at a wide circle of ground cleared of snow.

"Yes," Rick said. "He broke a branch from this bush and swept the snow away. We just have to be careful he's not on the lookout for us."

As the day grew to a close, Grady held up his hand and they came to a stop.

"We must be getting close now," he said. "Any ideas, men?"

Before anyone could reply, a shotgun blast cut the air.

Pow!

A boulder behind Danny exploded, and rocks and dust flew in his face. Rick grabbed the reins of Fire Eye and whipped him around.

Pow! Pow!

As shots rang out all around them, they dashed down the trail. Rick waved his hand and they followed his lead into a small canyon. The canyon wall was steep. The horses stepped down the snowy incline and then slid to the bottom of the canyon.

"Is anybody hurt?" Rick asked, when they reached the canyon floor.

"No," Danny said. "I'm all right."

"You?" Rick asked, turning to Grady.

"No, I'm fine. But I think Manny found us first."

"I think we've found their hideout, "Rick said. "They'll be coming after us. We're not safe here." He lifted himself from his saddle to get a better view. "Danny," he said, "climb the other wall and see what it looks like. And hurry, they might be on us any minute."

Danny jumped from Fire Eye and found a path between two big boulders. A patch of juniper trees grew near the top of the canyon. He grabbed the tree trunks and pulled himself to a rock overhang.

Afraid to shout and give away their location, Rick waved from below. Danny crouched in the shadows of the trees. *They might be anywhere,* he thought, remembering the surprise of the shotgun blasts.

The sun was setting to the west, coloring the sky with streaks of red and purple. As the sky darkened, Danny saw puffs of light rising from the direction of the shotgun fire.

That must be Manny's camp, he thought. He stood tall and stepped on a rock to get a better view.

"Whoa," he whispered aloud. He looked to Rick and Mr. Grady, staring at him from the canyon below. Then he turned his sight to Manny's hideout. Two lanterns hung above the gate to a fort. A group of Manny's men rode horses through the gate.

Behind one of Manny's men, riding on the back of the saddle, was Mrs. Grady. A dark sack covered her head.

Danny doubled his fists and clenched his teeth.

"Where is she?" he said aloud. "Where is Sarah?"

Soon another group of men rode through the gate. Danny spotted Sarah. Her head was covered by a black sack and her arms were wrapped around the waist of a slave trader. Danny closed his eyes and felt a shiver of anger pass through him.

When he opened them, the full scene of the fort spread out before him. His eyes grew big when he saw the size of it. Six buildings were surrounded by a fence made of thin tree trunks and patched together with mud.

The back wall of the fort was solid rock, a steep canyon wall. Smoke rose from the chimneys and a dozen men walked across the grounds.

When the men carrying Sarah and Mrs. Grady entered the fort, no one moved to help them. Only a few even glanced at the new prisoners.

This happens every day, thought Danny. *They aren't afraid of anyone.* Then another thought crossed his mind. *No wonder Manny wants to kill us so badly. He gets everything he wants. He didn't have to find another gang when the Gradys shot his men. He just rode back to his fort.*

Danny climbed to the floor of the canyon, where Rick and Grady waited.

"What did you find?" Grady asked. "Did you see Sarah?"

"Yes," said Danny. His voice was quiet and serious.

"Is she all right?"

"Yes," Danny nodded. "And I saw Mrs. Grady, too. They are both unhurt. They had sacks over their heads, so they couldn't see anything. But they are safe. For now."

"Oh, thank you, Lord," Mr. Grady said. He bowed his head and closed his eyes.

"What else did you see, Danny?" Rick asked.

"Manny has more than an outlaw gang," Danny said. "He has an army."

"How many men?"

"I saw twenty. But there are many more. And they don't live in a camp. They have a fort. Six buildings and a tall fence. The back wall of the fort is a canyon wall. It's steep and tall."

"Did you see any sign of men who might be coming after us?" Rick asked.

"No. I don't think they will look for us," said Danny. "They are not afraid of us. They think they scared us away."

The men sat in silence while a yellow slice of moon rose above them. They huddled their horses together to keep warm during the cold night. It was just three men in a small canyon so close to Manny and his army. And not far away, shaking with fear in Manny's fort, a mother and daughter clung to each other on a cabin floor.

Chapter 18
Grady's Army

"We can't stay here all night," Rick said. "Let's find a place to get some sleep."

He turned his horse away from the fort and rode through the narrow canyon. Grady and Danny followed close behind. Soon they found a grassy patch near the canyon wall.

"Must be an underground spring here," Rick said. "This would be a good place to settle. We can let the horses graze." They tied the horses to a dead tree trunk and spread their blankets on the soft ground.

"Rick," Danny said. "I want to stay awake and keep watch."

"Good thinking, Danny," Grady said. "I don't trust Manny to just let us go. I'll take the second watch. Wake me up in a few hours."

"Don't leave me out," Rick said. "And Danny?"

"I know what you are going to say," said Danny. "I will stay close to camp. I won't try to be a hero."

"Good boy!" Rick said.

Soon the men were snoring softly. The wall of the canyon was an easy climb. Danny settled on a boulder with a good view of both ends of the canyon. When he climbed atop a flat boulder, he could see the road leading to the fort.

An hour later, a wagon entered Manny's fort. It was met by a guard holding a lantern. Danny watched as the wagon came to a stop before the largest building.

Manny stepped through the door. He pointed to the rear of the wagon and waved his arms, giving orders. The driver climbed on the wagon and shoved six new prisoners from the wagon to the ground. The prisoners were tied at the wrists. They wore black sacks over their heads.

I know what that feels like, Danny thought.

More of Manny's men appeared. They dragged the prisoners to the canyon wall at the far end of the fort. They left the prisoners curled up on the ground. In less than half an hour, Manny's men returned to their sleeping quarters.

They didn't even leave a guard to watch over the prisoners, thought Danny. *I guess they warned them about trying to escape. Besides, the prisoners can't even see where they are.*

Danny leaped from the boulder, slid down the wall, and hurried to Rick and Grady.

"Wake up," he said, in as loud a whisper as he dared.

"What is it, Danny?" Rick asked.

"New prisoners. Come see."

Soon Rick and Grady followed Danny to the boulder overlook. At first they could see nothing. Then the clouds parted, and in the moonlight they saw the fort below.

"There," Danny said, pointing to the prisoners.

"Those are my men," Grady said. "My men are alive! How did they get here?"

"A wagon carried them, not long ago," Danny said. "Manny met the wagon. They left the men without a guard."

"Are you sure no one is watching them?" Rick asked.

"Yes. I saw everyone go back inside."

"We need to act soon," Rick said. "If we wait until morning, we won't have a chance."

"My wife and Sarah are in the fort too," Grady said. "We can't leave them to Manny."

"As long as they are in the fort, we don't have a chance," Rick said. "Manny has too many men. We don't have enough guns to fight them."

"Manny is a slave trader," said Grady. "The same wagon that brought my men in will carry them out, and soon. They won't do Manny any good here. He has to sell them."

"You might be right," Rick said. "Yes, if we can attack the wagon away from the fort, our odds of winning are better. Two guards on the wagon and three of us."

"I can climb down the canyon wall," Danny said. "I can get knives to the men. Then they can attack the drivers from behind."

"What about horses?" Grady asked. "My men will need horses."

"We can get horses from the wagon," Danny said.

"This will take a miracle," said Rick, "but I've seen more than one miracle in the past few months. Maybe we can find another one."

"Here, Danny," Grady said, handing Danny his knife. "The man with the silver belt buckle, his name is Greg. He's built like a stump, quick and strong. Give him my knife. And Danny?"

"Yes?"

"Tell him who you are before you get too close."

"I understand," Danny said.

"Who should get my knife?" asked Rick, handing it to Danny.

"Any of them will fight as long as they can stand," Grady said.

"Be sure to tell the men to hide the knives and wait," Rick said. "We'll be watching from the hills. When the wagons are far from the fort, that's the time to attack."

Danny nodded. He tied the knives to his ankles and soon was gone. He circled the fort, stopping often and listening for any sounds below.

In less than an hour, he reached the steep canyon wall at the rear of the fort. He knelt behind a boulder and waited. *If anyone saw me, I would hear shouting,* he thought. *They would be coming after me.*

Danny heard nothing. He slipped around the boulder and crawled to the edge of the canyon wall. The floor of the fort was at least a hundred feet below him. He saw no vines or bushes on the rock wall.

There's nothing to hold on to while I climb down.

But Danny Blackgoat had learned that when a problem seemed impossible to solve, he was not looking hard enough for the answer. He closed his eyes and reached for his leather pouch. He gripped it tight and thought of Sarah and her mother and father.

"They saved my life," he whispered to himself.

When he opened his eyes, he saw a shadow on the wall less than ten feet below. A small rock jutted out from the wall. He let his eyes roam down the canyon. Every few feet he spotted a small hole in the rocks. He saw thick brown roots of dead trees.

Anything for me to grip, he thought, moving his gaze all the way to the floor of the canyon. *If I do fall, I hope I'm close to the ground.*

He did not let himself think about what he would do if he were caught. Danny reached for the two knives, making sure they were tied tightly to his ankles. He looked one final time at the grounds of the fort.

Nothing but darkness. Now is the time.

He lay on the ground and turned over on his stomach until his feet fell over the edge of the cliff. He slowly pushed himself, inch by inch. With only his shoulders on the rock ledge, he looked below. He scooted a foot to his right. The rock was lined up below him.

I hope it's strong enough to hold me.

He closed his eyes and pushed away from the ledge. With his palms open and his fingers grabbing anything they could grip, he caught a thick root and stopped. His legs swung away from the canyon wall and Danny held tight. When he heard the slow crack of the wooden root, he let go. Ten feet later, his right hand slid against a sharp rock. The rock cut deep, but Danny ignored the pain and slung his shoulders onto the rock.

With blood streaming from his hand, he caught his breath. He now hung halfway down the canyon wall. He took a quick look over his shoulder at the ground below. Saying a quiet prayer, he let go of the rock.

Danny fell the final twenty feet and his feet struck a boulder as he landed. He rolled to the ground and lay on his back, staring at the dark sky. His hand was bleeding and his body was bruised and aching.

I can't stay here. I have to get up.

Hoping he had no broken bones, Danny slowly rose to his feet. He lifted his arms and leaned forward, clutching his knees. His eyes spotted a pile of dust by the boulder. Taking a handful of powdery rocks, he patted his hand to stop the bleeding. He ripped a sleeve from his shirt and wrapped it around his hand.

"Did you men hear that?" a voice shouted. Danny hid behind the boulder.

"What is it?" another man asked.

Danny had fallen among the prisoners, Mr. Grady's men. They turned their heads to Danny. In the dim light of the moon, Danny saw the strangest sight of his life—six men tied to steep canyon wall, with black sacks covering their heads.

"It's me, Danny Blackgoat," he said, stepping toward them. "I am here with Mr. Grady and a friend. We'll get you out of here. We have a plan. But we have to be quiet so we don't wake anybody up."

Danny found Greg and gave him Grady's knife. He gave Rick's knife to another of Grady's men.

"Hide the knives. Don't do anything till they put you on a wagon and you leave the fort. When you are far enough away, you'll hear us coming for you. Mr. Grady says for you to take the driver from behind. We'll be there for you."

"I don't like it," Greg said. "We can cut ourselves free and go now. Why should we wait and see what they'll do to us?"

"There are too many," said Danny, "and they have shotguns. We would not have a chance. And even if we did escape, they still have Sarah and Mrs. Grady."

"They are here?" Greg asked.

"Yes," Danny said. "Manny carried them here. We followed him. If we are smart, we can all stay alive."

"You know Manny will kill you if he catches you," Greg said. "Why are you doing this?"

"You saved my life. Now it's my turn," said Danny. "Stay quiet and we will all stay alive. Now, I am going to tell Mrs. Grady of the plan."

Chapter 19
Meeting Manny's Dog

"Mother," Sarah whispered.

"Shhh, Sarah. We don't want to wake up the guard." Sarah and her mother leaned against the cabin wall. They were tied at the wrists and ankles. A single guard slept on the floor by the door.

"What will they do to us?" Sarah asked.

"Don't think about that."

"I can't stop thinking about it, Mother. What happened to Dad?"

Her mother rolled over and faced Sarah. She lifted her arms and wrapped her palms around Sarah's cheeks. She kissed her on the forehead.

"Sarah, I will never give up hope. That is what we must do now. We must hope."

"Hope for what?"

"We must hope that your father is still alive. We must hope that he will find us."

"If anybody can find us, Daddy can," Sarah said. "I wish Danny Blackgoat was still with us. He would know what to do."

The guard made a loud snoring noise and rolled against the wall. Sarah and her mother froze. They waited for several minutes without moving. Soon the guard returned to his easy snores.

"I am sorry, Mother," Sarah whispered. Her mother patted her cheek and the two fell asleep.

Ten minutes later, her mother slipped her hand over Sarah's mouth.

"Sarah, wake up," she said. "Stay very quiet. I think you got your wish."

Sarah started to speak, but her mother held her hand over her mouth.

"Shhh. Just listen."

Sarah nodded.

"If you scream or say anything, you might get him killed. Lift your head and look through the window."

Sarah rolled over and looked through the cabin window. Danny Blackgoat met her gaze.

Sarah wanted to shout. She wanted to wave her arms. She wanted to dash through the door and hug her long lost friend. She did none of these things.

Instead, she bit her lip to keep from hollering. She blinked her bright eyes and smiled the biggest smile of her life. Danny waved at her. He pointed to the window and lifted his palms. Mrs. Grady rose to her knees. She carefully lifted the window.

"Do not do anything," Danny said. "I do not have long. Mr. Grady is alive. He and a friend of mine, Rick, are near. Your men have two knives. They are captured, too. They are here. They will wait till the wagons leave the fort. Then they will escape. Do not try to escape. But know that Mr. Grady and I will be there for you."

"Thank you so much," Mrs. Grady said. "It's so good to know my husband is alive."

Sarah leaned close to the window and whispered, "Good to know you are still alive, Danny Blackgoat."

"We will rescue you both. That is my promise to you," Danny said. "Now I have to go. Do nothing. Just wait."

As suddenly as he appeared, Danny was gone. Sarah's mother put her fingers to her lips. Sarah nodded. She and her mother were so excited that they lay with their eyes wide open for half an hour. When they finally returned to sleep, they dreamed of happier days on the Grady ranch.

Danny crept from the cabin to the canyon wall. Grady's men stood tied to the wall with the sacks over their heads.

"It's me again," Danny said to the men. "Mrs. Grady and Sarah are safe. They know the plan."

Danny stood at the bottom and stared at the steep wall before him. As he looked above, he was struck with a new problem.

"I was so worried about climbing down the wall," he said, "I never thought about getting out. I can never climb up this wall. I have to find another way."

Grady's men said nothing. They had their own plan.

Danny circled the fort, staying in the shadows. When he came to the wooden fence, he looked for any crack in the logs large enough for him to slip through. He spotted a tree covered with leaves.

Maybe I can climb the tree and jump over the wall.

He walked slowly beneath the tree. A long limb stretched over the fence of the fort. Danny didn't hesitate. He grabbed a lower limb and pulled himself up the tree trunk.

He was only a few feet from the top of the fence when he heard a low growl.

GRRRRR!

He tried to lift his leg and leap over the fence, but sharp teeth bit into his pant leg. He shook his leg, but the teeth gripped tight. Danny looked down into the mean eyes of a large black dog. He shook his leg again. The dog waved back and forth, clinging to his pants. Danny lost his grip and fell to the ground.

"Who's there?" someone shouted from the cabin. Danny recognized this voice.

"Nooo," he moaned. "Not now!"

Carrying a lantern high above his head, Manny stepped through the cabin door.

"What did you catch?" he said to his dog. "Killer, you got something?"

Killer stood over Danny. His face was six inches away. His teeth were sharp and his growl was low and mean. Danny knew that if he moved, even slightly, Killer would jump for his throat.

"Look what fell from the sky!" Manny said. "Don't I know you, boy? Didn't you lie to me and get my men killed?"

He kicked Danny in the ribs. Killer barked and looked to Manny, waiting for the order to attack.

"Down boy," said Manny. "This one is mine."

Danny wrapped his arms around his ribs and rolled away.

"Don't move till I say you can!" Manny shouted, kicking him again. "I can get good money for a young, strong man like you. But you can be my slave first. And if you're still alive, maybe then I'll sell you."

Manny knelt down and turned Danny's face to his. "You should have killed me when you had the chance," he said.

Those were the last words Manny ever spoke.

Chapter 20
The New Manny

Manny fell forward, his shirt covered in blood. Danny rolled away as his body struck the ground. The dog leaped for Danny but stopped in midair, jerked backward by a leash.

"You didn't think we could stay tied up, did you, Danny?" Greg said. While the dog growled and snapped his jaws, Greg gripped the leash around his neck.

"How did you know I was here?" Danny asked.

"We followed you, to make sure you were safe." Two more men stepped from the shadows. "Here," Greg said, handing the dog over, "tie this dog's mouth tight shut and leash him to a tree."

"Where are the other men?" asked Danny.

"They're close by," Greg said, "guarding the front of the cabin. Now we have to find a way out of the fort. We can't wait till they're ready to sell us. Everything changes now that Manny is dead."

Danny glanced at the dark puddle around Manny's head.

"It was him or you, and that was an easy choice to make," Greg said.

"Thank you," Danny said in a quiet voice.

"You're welcome. Now, any ideas?"

"I would never do this, but it might work," Danny said. "Everyone knows Manny by his hat. It's a dark night. You can wear his hat. Your shirt is dark, like his. Maybe tie his red bandana around your neck. Manny always wears it. We could all ride in the back of a wagon. The guards at the gate would never try to stop Manny."

The men looked at each other. Finally, Greg spoke.

"That's a big risk, riding a wagon right under their noses. But let's do it. No time to wait."

The men kicked dirt over the bloody ground. They rolled Manny on his back and removed his hat and bandana. "What should we do with his body?" a man asked.

"Toss it over the fence so they won't find it right away," Greg said.

Suddenly, a light appeared in the cabin. Greg reached for a stone at the base of the tree. He crept to the corner of the cabin. One of Manny's men, dressed in a long sleeping shirt, stepped to the front porch.

"Manny?" he called out. "What are you doing?"

"Here," Greg said, in a rough voice.

"That you, Manny?" the man asked, stepping around the corner. He was met with a stone to the side of his head. As he slumped to the ground, two men caught him and dragged him behind the cabin.

"No time to wait," Greg said. "We can't hide everybody. Tie him to the tree and let's find a wagon." In ten minutes a wagon with two young horses appeared, driven by Grady's men.

"I'll drive," said Greg. "Everybody get on. Let's go!"

"Wait!" Danny said.

"What is it? We have to go."

"Not without Sarah and Mrs. Grady," Danny said. "Give me five minutes. If I'm not back, go without me." Danny wished he could take back those words as soon as he spoke them.

He dashed across the grounds, hoping the guards at the gate would not spot him. When he reached the cabin window, he knocked softly. Mrs. Grady looked up.

Danny peered through the window. The guard was asleep on the far wall. Mrs. Grady saw the fear in Danny's face. He waved his hands at her, and she lifted the window.

Danny took her by the arm and leaned close to her ear.

"We go now," he said. Mrs. Grady touched Sarah and gently put her hand over her mouth.

"Shhh," she whispered, lifting her daughter to her feet.

They guard rolled over and snored loudly, but he didn't wake up. When Sarah and Mrs. Grady were standing beside him, Danny hurried to the shadows of the wall and motioned for them to follow. Sarah gasped when she saw Manny lying in a pool of blood.

"Climb on," Greg said. "Danny, sit behind me, but don't let them see you."

As they neared the gate, Greg pulled Manny's hat low over his forehead.

"Manny," a guard shouted. *"Todo esta bien?"*

Greg coughed and waved at the guard as the wagon passed through the gate. "Umm," he muttered, nodding his head and coughing into his fist.

The guard said nothing.

"That was too easy," Danny thought.

The thought had barely crossed his mind when a loud shotgun blast shattered a wheel of the wagon.

Chapter 21
Farewell to the Old

The wagon toppled on its side. Sarah screamed and the men scrambled to their feet, climbing through the rear of the wagon. A guard holding a lantern ran through the gate.

"We've got 'em now," he shouted. "They don't have any guns."

The loud crack of a rifle cut the air. Danny rolled to his feet in time to see the guard clutching his leg and falling. The lantern fell away and his shotgun flew from his hand.

"Danny, get his gun," Greg shouted. "Men, stay together. Use the wagon for cover."

Danny dashed to the fallen guard and took his rifle. As he turned away, another guard came through the gate on horseback.

Pow!

As the guard rode into the light of the lantern, another shotgun blast sent him falling to the ground. Danny looked up to see Rick and Mr. Grady, kneeling behind a boulder and aiming their guns at the gate. Soon a pair of Manny's men dashed through the gate to the fort. Two gun blasts later they joined the other fallen men, rolling in pain.

Who controls the gate controls the battle, thought Danny. *Manny built the fort so there was only one way in and one way out. We have already won!*

Less than half an hour after the firing started it was over.

A voice called out from the tower overlooking the gate.

"Hold your fire! Manny is gone. Nobody has to follow his orders anymore. Leave us alone and you can go."

"We need a wagon and horses!" Mr. Grady shouted.

"We will bring you both. Let us take care of our wounded, and we'll bring you a wagon and two horses."

Soon a wagon pulled by two strong horses rolled through the gate. Several of the guards hurried to their wounded friends and carried them inside the fort.

Rick hitched the horses to the new wagon. They soon pulled away from the fort, with Rick driving the wagon and Grady seated beside him. Some of Grady's men rode horses and some rode in the wagon with his family.

"Can we trust them?" Grady asked. "Will they leave us alone?"

"We can never let our guard down," said Rick. "But I think they'll let us go. If the truth be known, they're probably as glad to see Manny gone as we are."

They rode in silence until morning.

As the red rays of dawn colored the sky, Danny took a tiny pinch of corn pollen from his pouch and whispered his morning prayer. He closed his eyes and tossed the pollen from the rear of the wagon. A small gust of wind carried the pollen dust east, to the rising sun.

Sarah stretched her arms and sat up.

"Danny Blackgoat, are you here?"

"Yes," said Danny.

"Can you get us something to eat? I'm hungry."

"Sarah," said Mrs. Grady, "why are you asking him that?"

"Well, Mother," Sarah replied, "Danny rescued us from the fort and all those guards and slave traders. Bringing us something for breakfast should be easy!"

For the first time in a long week, the Gradys laughed. When the laughter settled, Rick looked at Mr. Grady and spoke quietly.

"Where do you want to go, Grady?"

"You need to get back to my ranch," Grady said. "Your supply wagon is there. They're probably waiting for you at Fort Davis. Isn't that where you were headed?"

"That seems like a lifetime ago," said Rick. "Yes, I'll get my wagon. But your home is burned. What do you plan on doing?"

"I still have my family and my men," said Grady. "And I don't think we have to worry about Manny's men for a while."

"Mr. Grady?" Danny spoke from behind the wagon seat.

"What is it, Danny?" Grady replied.

"If you want to rebuild your house and stay on the ranch," Danny said, "I'll help you. I can stay at the ranch for now and Rick can take me to see my family when he passes through. That would be safer for me than hiding out by the fort."

Mr. Grady and Rick looked at each other without speaking. They shared the same thought: *This young man understands more than he should for his age.* Their eyes shone with admiration for Danny Blackgoat.

"I will need to ask the lady in charge," said Grady.

"That would be fine with me," said Mrs. Grady.

"I'm not talking about you," Mr. Grady said. "I'm talking about Sarah."

Once more, soft laughter filled the wagon.

Sarah took a deep breath before replying.

"Let me think for a minute," she finally said. "Danny Blackgoat can stay with us on one condition."

"What condition?" Danny asked.

"No scalping!" Sarah shouted. "I don't want any haircut, from you or your grandmother."

"I'm not telling my grandmother what to do," Danny said.

"Good thinking," said Mr. Grady.

"You're learning," said Rick.

In the silence that followed, Danny thought of his family. *My grandfather was right. I am too close to death. I wish I could be with them again, leading my sheep to the spring at Canyon de Chelly.*

His thoughts followed the rugged road of the past year. They stopped when he remembered his old friend. *I hope Jim Davis is safe.*

Jim Davis was safe. Even after Danny Blackgoat had escaped Fort Davis on a stolen horse, no one had suspected Jim Davis of helping him. He had the trust of the officers at the fort, and he was the best carpenter they'd ever seen.

"We're going to miss that old man," said the officer in command. He held a telegraph in his hand.

"Jim Davis is being transferred to Fort Sumner," he announced to his officers at their morning meeting. "I hope he gets along with Navajos."

About the Author

Tim Tingle is an Oklahoma Choctaw and an award-winning author and storyteller. Every Labor Day, Tingle performs a Choctaw story before Chief Gregory Pyle's State of the Nation Address, a gathering that attracts over ninety thousand tribal members and friends.

In June 2011, Tingle spoke at the Library of Congress and presented his first performance at the Kennedy Center, in Washington, DC. From 2011 to the present, he has been a featured author and storyteller at Choctaw Days, a celebration at the Smithsonian's National Museum of the American Indian honoring the Oklahoma Choctaws.

Tingle's great-great grandfather, John Carnes, walked the Trail of Tears in 1835.

In 1992, Tim retraced the Trail to Choctaw homelands in Mississippi and began recording stories of tribal elders. His first book, *Walking the Choctaw Road*, was the outcome. His first children's book, *Crossing Bok Chitto*, garnered over twenty state and national awards and was an Editor's Choice in the *New York Times* Book Review.

As an instructor at the University of Oklahoma, Tingle presented summer classes at Santa Fe, New Mexico. Fueled by his own family's survival on the Trail of Tears, he became fascinated with the Navajo Long Walk, and the Danny Blackgoat series came to life.

PathFinders novels offer exciting contemporary and historical stories featuring Native teens and written by Native authors.

For more information, visit:
NativeVoicesBooks.com

Danny Blackgoat, Navajo Prisoner
Tim Tingle
- 978-1-939053-03-9
- $9.95
- 160 pages

Tribal Journey
Gary Robinson
978-1-939053-01-5 •
$9.95 •
120 pages •

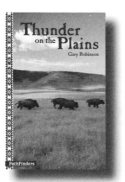

Thunder on the Plains
Gary Robinson
- 978-1-939053-00-8
- $9.95
- 128 pages

Available from your local bookstore or you can buy them directly from:

Book Publishing Company • P.O. Box 99 • Summertown, TN 38483
1-800-695-2241

Please include $3.95 per book for shipping and handling.